Andrew Robertson

The Kidnapped Squatter and Other Australian Tales

Andrew Robertson

The Kidnapped Squatter and Other Australian Tales

ISBN/EAN: 9783337070526

Printed in Europe, USA, Canada, Australia, Japan

Cover: Foto ©Andreas Hilbeck / pixelio.de

More available books at **www.hansebooks.com**

The Kidnapped Squatter

AND OTHER AUSTRALIAN TALES

PRINTED BY
SPOTTISWOODE AND CO., NEW-STREET SQUARE
LONDON

THE

KIDNAPPED SQUATTER

AND OTHER AUSTRALIAN TALES

BY

ANDREW ROBERTSON

LONDON
LONGMANS, GREEN, AND CO.
AND NEW YORK : 15 EAST 16th STREET
1891

CONTENTS

PAGE

THE KIDNAPPED SQUATTER 3

ALL FOR GLITTERING GOLD 41

JACK REEVELEY 93

A BUSH ADVENTURE 216

THE KIDNAPPED SQUATTER

B

CHAPTER 1

WILLIAM BALCKE was a squatter, who had settled in Victoria about six years before our tale commences. He had been one of that numerous class of reckless, extravagant, uncalculating, ne'er-do-weels who squander the paternal property, who drink the family plate, who eat the family residence, who gamble away fair fields and ancient halls, and who race away anything else they can lay hands on, with a speed surpassing that of the most famous Voltigeur, Flying Dutchman, or Will-o'-the-Wisp. While money or credit lasted, all went smooth and well and 'merry as a marriage bell;' and, as a certain scarlet hero sang, 'How happy the soldier who lives on his pay, And spends half a crown out of sixpence a day!' Like that heroic youth, he thought it would last for ever, and that the weather would be always bright and fair, and friends be true and Jews prove kind. But he was miserably disappointed. He was doomed to

B 2

feel the gripe of poverty, and also that of the bailiff.
He knew what it was to have his coat buttoned to
the throat in the warmest weather, and, in short,
had passed through all the phases of want and
wretchedness. While in this miserable situation
he reproached himself bitterly for his foolishness,
and determined to regain the position he had lost
—to mount again the height from which he had
fallen, and to lead a different life.

Just in the midst of his good resolutions a
small legacy was left him by a distant relative,
which although small seemed to him a munificent
and princely sum.

With this money in his pocket, and double its
value in experience stowed away somewhere, he
determined to begin the world anew. He chose the
colony in which our scene is laid as the most likely
place in which to better his prospects, and here he
arrived in the year 1840. He leased a small
station, stocked it with sheep and cattle, throve
apace, and at the period when our tale begins was
one of the most extensive squatters in the country.

His homestead was situated at no very great
distance from Portland, in one of those lovely
valleys which are so numerous in that district.
His house was managed by a lady-like woman, who

was apparently about twenty-six years old. Her name was Fanny Roundley. Her complexion was fair, clear and transparent, her features were small and delicately moulded, her eyes were blue, and her hair was golden. She managed her household duties in an admirable manner, and attended to the comfort of Balcke in every particular. She became so useful to him as to be almost indispensable. She kept his accounts and paid his bills. She was eyes, and hands, and head to him. Was he late in getting home, she welcomed him at the door. Was he melancholy, her ready smile recalled his wonted cheerfulness; or was he sick, she nursed him tenderly.

But, notwithstanding her apparent kindness and disinterested regard for his personal welfare, she did not escape the lynx eyes of certain envious gossipers, who were sceptical—very sceptical—and said many sharp things, and poured forth as much vinegar regarding her as would have set Fanny's teeth on edge had she heard them. Gossip further said that she was a 'designing woman, an artful hussy, and a deep dissimulator,' and that 'she was setting her cap at him.' She paid great attention to her personal appearance, and really dressed with much taste. She spent most of her money on silks, satins, flowers, feathers, tulle, lace, ribbons, and other articles too numerous to mention, to adopt the words of the puffing advertisers. All in good taste and keeping, nevertheless. Gossip further said that the flowers were as real as her affection, the lace as transparent as her designs, and the tulle as flimsy as her disguises.

Balcke very soon began to view her in the same light as her detractors. His keen perception enabled him to detect the many little tricks and artifices by which she sought to gain his esteem and affection. She praised him too profusely, attended him too much, and smiled upon him too sweetly.

With all Fanny's exertions she seemed to make no progress in the attack on the citadel of his heart—his adamantine heart, his obdurate heart. Her heaviest artillery was brought to bear on it; her utmost skill was put forth. She found that flattery would not do it, that ribbons and laces would not do it, that the sweetest of smiles would not do it, and that everything else she had tried could not make her succeed. She had exhausted all her ideas; she had played her trump card.

But, what was worse than all, he began to absent himself from home, and was often to be found at Mr. Hardcliffe's, a neighbouring squatter, who had some lovely daughters, one of whom had captivated him, made a conquest of him, and held him in thrall.

This was too much for Fanny to bear. She forthwith, seeing the hopelessness of the pursuit, transferred her affections to Jack Blake, the overseer, and led him captive at her will.

'Jack,' said Fanny, one evening, 'do you know that I am going to leave the station? I had a conversation with Balcke last night, and he told me it would be better for all parties that I should go. He said he would soon be married, and that the hussy he was going to bring here would want my room, and he did not wish to have a housekeeper any longer. He made many other excuses of the same kind, but I am determined not to be put aside in this manner; I who have tended him in sickness and in health, and managed all his affairs better than he could have done—and thus to be cast off like a worn-out ribbon. I won't stand it, and can't bear it, and shan't, I can tell you.'

'Well, Fanny,' said Jack, 'if you'll be guided by me, I will put you on a scheme, a bright scheme; and, you know, all is fair in love and war. He wants to put you aside for the sake of one who, perhaps, does not care a jot about him, and who, I'll be bound, only cares about his money. Now, as you can't get him, I don't see why you should not get some of his cash. You helped to make it. Besides, he has got plenty and will never miss it.'

'But how am I to get it?' said Fanny.

'Will you never divulge what I am going to tell you?' said Jack.

'No, never.'

'Will you swear it?'

'Yes.'

'On the Bible?'

'Yes.'

'Well, the scheme is this. We must start for Portland to-morrow, and get married as soon as possible. I'll personate Balcke, and sign his name. I can write it so that he could not tell whether he wrote it or not.'

'But what good will that do?' said Fanny.

'Look here,' and Jack thereupon pulled out a large pair of false whiskers and moustaches, and

fitted them to his own face. He then produced a
wig and put it on, and, thus accoutred, nineteen
out of twenty would have mistaken him for Balcke,
especially at a little distance. In features he was
not unlike. Balcke had dark hair, he had light.
Balcke wore whiskers and moustaches, Jack had
shaved clean for some months.

'You see,' said Jack, 'I have prepared a surprise
for you. I have revolved my scheme in my own pate
for some months. Now, don't I look like Balcke ? '

'I own you do, somewhat ; but what good will
that do ? '

'You shall see. We shall see. I will explain
all to-morrow, for it is getting late.'

And he accordingly explained all in the morning.

CHAPTER II

IT was one of those hot and dusty days which are so oppressive to Europeans. The herbage was burnt up, the swamps and creeks were dry, the cattle lay sleeping in the deepest shade, the air seemed on fire, and all nature was in a burning fever; its pulse throbbed, and its breath was heavy and hot. The ground was parched and cracked, and the fissures looked as beseechingly as Dives did for a drop of water.

Fanny and Jack emerged from the house about midday, and, after quietly saddling their horses, they rode along at a slow pace through a dense forest, which served in some measure to screen them from the fierce rays of the sun. They wore thick veils, which would completely hide their features from the gaze of any travellers they might chance to meet.

When they had proceeded a short distance on

their journey, they left the beaten track and struck across the forest.

Immense flocks of parrots and cockatoos took flight; lizards hastily hid themselves under fallen trees, or ran up the boles of the growing timber; snakes peered out of their dens and slunk away; and iguanas scuttled up the trees, as the two travellers wended their way through the densely timbered country. Thousands of mosquitoes assailed them at every vulnerable point; routed in front, the attack was renewed in the rear with redoubled fury, and, dislodged in that quarter by a brilliant series of manœuvres, incessant charges were made simultaneously and tumultuously on every side. Detached companies lay in ambush under every tree, bush, and boulder, and charged horse and biped with a determination and courage worthy of a better cause. The poor horses suffered severely; their tails had been ruthlessly shorn, and they were completely defenceless and at tho mercy (if they had any of that scarce quality) of their bloodthirsty foes.

The sun was setting as they emerged from the forest. The sky was a mass of glory. Pinnacles, columns, domes, towers, and battlements of cloud were heaped in grand confusion, like a poet's dream, round the departing orb of day. The nearer distance was soon submerged in gloom, and the cold blue shadows were toiling up the mountain peaks, like travellers who haste to have their journey over before the close of day.

Fanny and Jack had now regained the main track, and soon arrived at their destination. They put up at the —— Hotel, a small hostelry which has long since passed away. Fanny was much fatigued, so, after a slight supper, she retired for the night.

As soon as she had retired, Jack, whiskered and moustached, sallied out. He walked along at a brisk pace until he came to the unpretending wattle and daub cottage of the Rev. Silas Snuff-much, the worthy minister of the Scotch Kirk. He knocked at the door, which was opened by a dried-up, withered old mummy of a servant.

'Is't the minister you want, man?' said the old woman. 'I'm thinking you'll find him wi' his books, puir man, if you'll gang in this way;' and so saying she opened the door of the minister's bedroom, breakfast-room, dining-room, and study. The minister was a lonely man, bachelor, aged fifty.

The Rev. Silas Snuffmuch sat in an old-fashioned easy-chair poring over an old tome, oblivious of everything else mundane. I do not know whether or not the lines had fallen unto him in pleasant places, but they seemed to have concentrated themselves more particularly about the corners of the eyes and mouth, and down the sides of the cheeks; as if the pleasant streams of life had long since ebbed, and had only left the ripple mark on the sands of time. There was a dark brown spot under his nose, and his clerical neck-band, and what shirt-front was visible, were powdered over with the same colour.

'Good evening,' said Jack, as he entered. 'Good evening,' he repeated. The minister shook himself, took a good pinch of snuff, and then, and not till then, did he return the salutation. In the meantime Jack had seated himself in the only other chair the room could boast.

'Warm weather this, doctor,' said Jack.

'It is even so,' said the Rev. Silas. 'Nevertheless,' he added, 'I felt it not, for my soul communed not with the things of this present; for being, as it were, absent from the body, the heat of the day made itself not manifest corporeally—that is to say, in the flesh.'

'My name is Balcke,' said Jack, 'of Quagu-rackjcp, and I wish you to marry me to-morrow night, in your own house.'

It may be mentioned that a minister of the Scotch Kirk will marry at any time of the day or night.

'Yea, verily,' said the minister. 'But, as it is a serious, solemn, and important step you are about to take, suffer me to tender you one word of exhortation.'

The doctor had only uttered a few syllables of the 'one word,' when Jack leant back in his chair and his head drooped on his breast, for he was tired and sleepy. He vainly endeavoured to keep awake, but soon he nodded and swayed to and fro like a bulrush.

The Rev. Silas Snuffmuch went on with the 'one word' for a full hour. Jack nodded every minute or so, 'approving and assenting in the usual manner,' as the worthy clergyman after-wards related in the simplicity of his heart. He thought he had now impressed his visitor with the full importance of the serious and solemn step he was about to take, and had just cleared his throat for a grand final effort, when Jack gave a nod of more than usual energy, and awoke just in time to hear the last sentence, which was delivered with great earnestness and gravity.

'God, who searcheth the hearts and trieth the reins of all men, knoweth the motives which prompt you to enter the holy.state of matrimony. He also knoweth that we are dust, and will never leave us nor forsake us.'

Jack then took leave, and wended his way back to the hotel.

True to appointment, Jack and Fanny arrived at the minister's house two hours after sundown next evening. They found the Rev. Silas waiting to receive them. The necessary documents were lying on the table, and the business in hand was proceeded with at once. After the preliminary forms had been completed, and the witnesses who had been secured for the occasion had signed their names, the doctor read them a long and impressive admonition. He afterwards offered up an earnest prayer for a blessing on their union, which done, he advanced to the bride, and in a few observations, which were meant to be facetious, wished her much happiness in her married life. He then dismissed them with his blessing, and they went their way.

There was a crushing weight at their hearts.

Avarice and revenge were running riot. Their consciences smote loud and strong. The Spirit of Evil was urging them on, and whispering 'All is well,' but fear and doubt beset them on every side. Every sound was a terror, and every sigh of the calm ocean breeze filled them with alarm. The Spirit of Good was also lifting up his voice, by entreaty and warning, but it was stifled, unheeded, and uncared for.

They left Portland the same night, and travelled swiftly until they arrived near the station, about day-break. Jack had by this time removed his wig and moustaches, and he rode forward and got his horse stabled before anyone was stirring, and then he quietly crept to bed. Fanny did not make her appearance until about midday, and no one took any notice of her arrival. Balcke was absent from home, and the people were attending to their ordinary duties, so that, if she wished for conceal-ment, she had no difficulty in accomplishing her object.

'Where secrecy or mystery begins, vice or roguery is not far off.'

About a week after the marriage took place, Jack rode up to the home-station and informed Balcke that one of the shepherds at an out-station had been found dead, and that the sheep had got among the scrub and were in danger of being lost.

Balcke took horse immediately, and galloped off, accompanied by Jack, to the out-station. He ordered the men out to recover the sheep, and he and Jack went with them to give their assistance and advice.

The sun had set before they arrived at the scrub, but as the moon was rising they determined to go on with the search. Balcke declared that he would remain with them all night.

'What is the use of you remaining?' said Jack. 'Your horse is of no use in the scrub, and we can do no good here.'

''Deed yes, maister, ye had better gang hame to your ain fireside,' said an old one-armed Scotch shepherd. 'It's no canny to be out sae late at e'en, and I'se warrant ye I'll hae every fleece at the huts before mornin'.'

'No, no,' said Balcke, 'I'll dismount, and give the men every assistance in my power.'

'Well, well,' said Jack impatiently, 'a wilful man must have his way; but take a pull at my flask, and that may keep away the bad effects of the damp night air.'

Balcke took a long draught, for he felt the air cold and raw.

They commenced the search, and soon found some of the sheep ; as they penetrated the scrub they got a considerable number more, and consigned them to the care of two men.

Balcke very soon complained to Jack that he felt very drowsy, so much so as to be hardly able to keep his eyes open.

'Oh!' said Jack, 'take another pull at the brandy ; if it does not keep you awake, you will, at least, sleep all the sounder when you get home. If you ever get there,' Jack added mentally.

'You had better go home now,' said Jack ; 'you can't bear the fatigue, and the men have found most of the sheep.'

'I think I had better,' said Balcke, in a very drowsy tone, and with a decided hiccup.

'I think so too,' said Jack, with a triumphant air.

Jack assisted him on his horse, and they both rode slowly homeward.

'I ca-an't tell why I a-am so ve-very sleepy.'

'Oh!' said Jack, 'that is of easy explanation. The planetary influences affect the brain at a right angle triangle, and the moon's beams weave a tangled web, and those who have to do with sheep will become sheepish, for your brains have gone a wool-gathering.'

'You're d-d-d-drunk,' said Balcke, who by this time seemed quite stupefied, and his head had sunk on his breast. Jack was obliged to hold him on his horse. 'D-d-d-drunk,' he muttered again, in an oblivious tone.

'Mynheer Van Dunck, he oft got drunk, and he drank twelve bottles a day, and the landlord swore he was a dirty skunk, for he had no money to pay,' roared Jack at the top of his voice.

The fact was that Jack had been taking sundry secret draughts from a flask which he carried attached to his saddle, and the liquor was showing itself in the boisterous and devil-may-care manner which he now exhibited. Balcke, on the contrary, was quite stupefied, and seemed almost inanimate, the brandy he had drunk having been drugged by Jack, the better to carry out the project which he and Fanny had planned. But I am anticipating.

Jack was obliged to ride close to Balcke, and hold him by one arm, so as to keep him from falling. He led the horses towards the sea, in the direction of the caves, a remarkably picturesque and singular locality, where they soon arrived.

Jack pulled Balcke from his saddle, and laid him on the ground. He then untied a coil of rope from his horse's neck, and wound it round Balcke's body, and by its means lowered him into the deepest and most precipitous cave. He then cut the rope, and threw it down into the darkness and gloom—into the living sepulchre; as chief mourners drop the rich and glossy cords and tassels, which fall dull and mournful on the narrow house of those they loved so well.

He left the spot and mounted his horse, taking Balcke's animal with him. He rode slowly along, peering as he went into every bush and behind every tree. An intense feeling of fear had taken possession of him. An owl flapped its wings and uttered its doleful cry close above his head, which made him quake and quiver like a dancing dervish during the lull of one of his paroxysms. The blood forsook his cheeks and rushed to his heart in a burning stream. His hair stood on end with terror —at all events, it stood as much on end as it was capable of doing. Some owls hooted in a clump of trees near him, and when he looked among the branches his heated imagination conjured up on every gnarled bough the most horrible imps, who seemed to chatter and mock him with a hollow laugh, as he passed along. One more real than the rest tumbled down, and immediately scrambled up the tree as fast as his legs would carry him, his grey bushy tail whisking about his head all the while.

He did not feel at ease until he had got into the plain and had left the forest far behind.

He took Balcke's horse and tied him to a small solitary tree, where the scrub was about three feet high. He then proceeded in the direction of where he left the men. He had not gone far before he dismounted. He struck a match and set fire to the grass. The flames immediately shot up, for everything was as dry as tinder, and ran along the ground in the direction of the caves. In a short time the fire had reached the brushwood and scrub and was raging in the forest near the sea.

And it raged in its fury, leaping from spray to branch, and from branch to bough. It hissed, and sputtered, and crackled, and groaned, and moaned, and howled, and revelled, and rioted in the depths of the forest, and it lapped the waters with its fiery tongue. Cries of eloquent woe filled the air ; its march was a march of death, and the forest denizens sang their own sad requiem.

Jack did not stay to see the effects of the fire,

but galloped off, and in half an hour had gained the scrub, and found the men about to return with a number of the sheep. They had seen the fire, but thought nothing of it—an occurrence which had been so common that summer. - Jack told them he had left Balcke about half-way home, and had returned at his request. He then accompanied the men to the out-station, and remained there until late next day.

When he reached the homestead he said he wished to see Balcke, and asked the men where he was. When they told him that he had not returned he seemed much astonished, and told them how he had left their master the night before on his way home, and could not see what had become of him.

Some one suggested that he might have lost himself in the scrub, or been overtaken by the fire, or that he might have changed his mind, and stayed at some of the huts instead of making for home.

'Very likely,' said Jack, 'for he was uncommonly tired and sleepy, and could hardly keep his eyes open. Tom,' said he, addressing one of the men, 'if he does not come back to-night, you had better take a horse and ride round to the out

stations, and see if you can't hear something of
him. He can't be lost in the scrub, for he knows
the country as well as a dingo, and he could not
have been overtaken by the fire, for that was near
the sea, and he had no occasion to go within miles
of it.'

When Fanny heard that Balcke was missing,
she understood the matter at once. She openly
and ostentatiously feigned great distraction of
mind, while she inwardly rejoiced. She wept and
sobbed hysterically, and ran wildly about, asking
tidings of her 'poor lost husband.' The men
stared when she said 'husband,' but that was all,
for rumours were abroad that she had been married
privately to Balcke, which rumours were industri-
ously circulated by Fanny herself. She refused to
be comforted and said she would go and look for him.

Jack went up to her and persuaded her to go
back to the house, promising that everything
would be done which could be thought of.

'Well, Fanny,' said Jack, when they had got
back to the house, 'the deed is done. He is in
the cave hard and fast; there he must remain until
we are beyond his reach. In the meantime, after
the hue-and-cry has subsided, you can apply for
letters of administration and all that sort of thing.

He has no relations, so there will be no difficulty or bother in the matter.'

Next day Tom was despatched to the out-stations, and returned without any tidings of his lost master. A messenger was sent off to the two nearest squatters, with the news that Balcke was lost in the bush, and that his wife earnestly requested their assistance.

'Who the d—— is his wife?' said Mr. Hardcliffe, the father of Balcke's affianced bride, who was first appealed to by Tom.

'Oh, Miss Roundley, who kep' his house,' said the man.

'The d——,' said Mr. Hardcliffe; 'if you joke with me, sir, I'll break every bone in your body. When were they married, and who married them?' he continued almost choking with passion, for he saw by the man's face that it was no joke.

'I dunno, but Jack Blake, the overseer, told me himself, and he oughter know sure—ly, that they were married by old Snuffmuch, at Portland, in a clandescript or private manner—them's the very words he said—and says he, "You needn't say anything to nobody," says he. "Can a duck swim?" says I.'

Mr. Hardcliffe slammed the door in the man's

face, and he muttered, as he did so, that Balcke
might starve in the bush for anything he cared.

The man was more successful at the other
station, and he returned with the intelligence that
a large party would be over in the morning, to
commence the search.

Early next morning a number of horsemen
arrived, and with them was Mr. Hardcliffe, who
had somewhat relented when he thought that the
life of a fellow mortal was at stake. Jack had
mustered all the men on the station, and they
were ready to set out. He rode up to meet the
horsemen, and proposed that he and the men
should search the country for twelve miles along
the seashore, and suggested that Mr. Hardcliffe
with his party should disperse over the plains,
while Mr. Horker and his men should scour the
country to the north. To this they agreed, and
immediately rode away to the different parts of
the country allotted them.

Jack and his party searched under every fallen
tree, and peered through the bushes. No one
hought of going near the caves, as they were so
far from the point where Balcke was last seen,
according to Jack's account. After a long time
one of the men found Balcke's horse. He cooeyed,

and they all rushed up. There lay all that was left of the poor brute. A few charred bones, some half-melted rings, buckles and stirrups, were all that remained to show the fate of poor Dample.

The animal must have been severely burnt before the rope was sufficiently scorched to allow it a chance of escape. Mad with pain and fright, the poor horse must have rushed headlong to destruction—into the very middle of the fire, where it was, no doubt, suffocated first, and then burnt to a cinder.

Now that the remains of the horse were found, the fate of Balcke could admit of little doubt. Traces of him could not be far off, and the search was kept up until night. No indication could be found. Jack said that it was almost impossible that his remains would ever be seen, as his charred bones would be mingled with the fallen trunks of trees, and the still smoking embers.

When they got home they found that Mr. Hardcliffe and his men had returned without success. Later in the night Mr. Horker and his party arrived, and, of course, they were equally unsuccessful. When Jack and his men told how they had found the charred bones of the horse, in the manner described, their hearts sank within them, and they felt that there was no hope whatever of seeing their old friend again.

Both Mr. Horker and Mr. Hardcliffe agreed that it was useless to renew the search, as far as they, at least, were concerned, and that their best course was to set off in the morning for their respective homes, leaving Jack and his men to follow up the discovery they had made, in the hope of finding poor Balcke's remains.

To this Jack agreed, and to tell the truth he was only too glad to get rid of them so easily.

The two gentlemen and their men left on the following morning. Jack and his party went back to the forest and spent another fruitless day. The next day was passed over in the same manner, and the next, and next. The men by this time were thoroughly tired of it, and Jack declared that it was labour in vain, and worse than useless, to do any more in the matter. They had done all that men could do. It was clear that Balcke had perished in the flames; for, as the horse could not escape, it was evident that its rider could not, and so they went back to their usual work, and gave themselves no further trouble.

In a week Balcke was as completely out of their minds as if they had never seen him or known him as a kind master.

CHAPTER III

In carrying out the incidents of a crime, we often find that the most consummate cunning and address are employed. Men who have never displayed the slightest foresight in the ordinary business of life, who have never been able to overcome common difficulties, will yet, in the prosecution of crime, show many of the best qualities man can possess. Determination, perseverance and forethought seem to be inherent in their minds, and sound judgment, well-weighed schemes and complete success seem to show that they have capacities of a high order. But when the work is accomplished—the crime committed—these qualities leave them altogether. The teachings of evil point out easy and safe methods of attaining the ends in view. They accept the offered guidance. They slavishly obey. They follow the evil promptings until the nefarious transaction is accomplished, or the bloody deed is done; then they are left in a maze—a tangled web—they are at their wit's end, and they have no power to extricate themselves. Their crimes find them out, and the strong arm of the law punishes them as they righteously deserve.

But to return to Balcke. He lay in a profound sleep until the night after he had been lowered into the cave. He then showed signs of returning consciousness. He stretched his benumbed limbs, shook himself, and tossed uneasily about, and groaned and grunted in a very lugubrious and doleful fashion. The drugged brandy had quite stupefied him. Jack the Giant-killer might have blown a blast loud enough to wake the dead, but it would not have roused him, and the roar of Niagara, supplemented by a score of modern Xantippes, would have been futile and vain.

Presently there were more decided indications of vitality. He slowly and painfully opened his eyes, and stared around him with amazement.

The moon was shining in all her splendour, and her rays lighted up the cave with a fairylike and weird effect, throwing out a delicate tracery here, sobering down an obtrusive pillar there, and casting a dim and holy light over the higher parts, while all below was bathed in gloom.

His heart beat furiously, his pulse throbbed and

his brain was burning. Where was he? Was he dreaming, was it all hallucination? He shut his eyes, expecting that all would vanish before he again opened them. But no! the same columns, the same mouldings, the same tracery met his gaze. It was no dream, it was real. There was the moon, gazing calmly and gently upon him; there were the stars peering at him, and twinkling as if tired of their nightly vigils; and there were the clouds, with their seemingly wan and solemn faces, as they looked at him and flitted past, while others glided up, gazed on him, and vanished one by one.

He fell asleep, and dreamt of his childhood. His sainted mother was near him, weeping and wailing. Great drops of agony fell from her meek eyes on his bronzed face, and she clasped him in her fond embrace and gently soothed him.

When he awoke the sun was shining through the opening of the cave in a sufficiently powerful manner to enable him to see the nature of his prison. He was lying under the cave's mouth, at a depth of some forty feet. How he had got there he could not tell. All that he remembered was that he had mounted his horse with the intention of riding home; he also knew that he had drunk repeatedly from Jack's brandy-flask. Afterwards, all was a blank.

Gradually he realised his position. How came the rope to be so carefully and securely tied round his chest, loins, and thighs? He must have been lowered into the cave by some one. Who did it? Who bore him malice? Whom had he offended? What motive could any one possibly have for so cruel and purposeless a deed?

Thus he questioned; the more he thought of the matter the more puzzled he became. Here was a deep mystery which he had no power to unravel. A cruel and lingering death was in store for him. Already he fancied that death was lurking near, anxiously watching the few remaining sands that were swiftly running down, and with uplifted scythe ready to strike.

Hope—the lighthouse on the reefs of life—which has guided many a crazy bark into a harbour of refuge, began to whisper that there might be a way of escape. There were passages branching off in all directions. He unloosed the rope and slowly rose, for his limbs were swollen and benumbed. He then explored the cave in all directions, but all was dark and gloomy.

At length, thoroughly exhausted, he threw himself down, where he had found himself on awaking. In doing so he fell against a small basket, which, on examination, was found to contain what seemed to him a great store of bread, meat, eggs, biscuits, &c. He took a piece of bread in one hand and meat in the other, and had eaten a considerable quantity before a thought passed through his mind as to the strangeness and opportuneness of the discovery. When he had fully appeased his appetite, which was not very soon, he quenched his thirst at a clear and ample stream, which flowed through the cave.

Fanny and Jack congratulated themselves meanwhile on the success of their scheme. Balcke was in their power. The neighbouring squatters believed him to be dead. A paragraph appeared in the Melbourne newspaper headed, 'Fire in the bush. Finding of the remains of a horse, and probable death of J. W. Balcke, Esq., who was last seen riding the animal.' There was a notice in another column : 'Died.—On the 3rd inst., J. W. Balcke, Esq., of Quagurackjep, having perished in a bushfire. His sorrowing widow mourns his loss.'

Fanny arrayed herself in widow's weeds, and assumed all the outward signs of grief.

In a short time notice was given that letters of administration would be applied for, and in the meantime the sheep and cattle were sold as rapidly as possible. Flock after flock and herd after herd were disposed of, and in a very brief period some thousands of pounds were collected.

Now that the conspiracy had turned out so well, and as the risk of discovery was continually before their eyes, they made up their mind to decamp with the booty.

It has been well said by the sacred penman, ' The wicked flee when no man pursueth.' This is true, for when a crime has been committed the guilty persons are constantly afraid of being brought to justice. They are frightened at shadows, and alarmed at the squeak of a mouse. Their accusing consciences irresistibly goad them on, putting ' sleep from their eyes and slumber from their eyelids,' and peace and quiet far from them. Anxiety preys on the mental, and fever, as a consequent, on the physical structure. The joys of life are sapped, and the foundation of all happiness is destroyed.

About a month after Balcke had disappeared Fanny went to Portland, and took passage for Melbourne in a small coaster. It was given out that her presence was necessary at the metropolis, in order to expedite some legal matters touching the letters of administration. Jack followed her in a

D

few days. He told the people in the neighbourhood that he was going to the north, to complete the purchase of a small station ; and that, as Mrs. Balcke intended to sell her run, he would commence stockholding on his own account. Instead of going north, however, he steered his way across country, in the direction of Melbourne, where he arrived the day after Fanny got into Hobson's Bay.

A vessel bound for England was just about to put to sea. They secured cabins, and got on board as the anchor was being weighed. The sailors sang cheerily, and all was bustle and confusion. They ran to their cabins, and Jack wrote the following letter in a feigned hand :

'A. S. Hardcliffe, Esq., Wappinhopley,
      viâ Portland.

'Sir,—I beg to inform you that Mr. Balcke is not dead, as has been supposed. The writer of this saw him alive and well, a week ago. You will find him down the Cathedral Cave, a hundred yards from Brazenchin Head. Burley Bill, the shepherd, knows the place well.—Yours truly,

'A FRIEND.'

Fanny wrote to Burley Bill, imploring him to go to the cave, where he would find Mr. Balcke alive. Having sealed the letters, Jack ran on deck, and asked the shipping clerk to take them ashore and post them at once. One or both must go all right, so Jack said to Fanny. Balcke would be rescued, and after all no great harm would be done.

Balcke was found in due course. A liberal supply of provisions had been furnished to him by some unseen hand. He was nothing worse for his long imprisonment; but, to add to his misfortunes, Miss Hardcliffe refused to see him, believing him to be married, and all his denials and protestations were treated with contempt.

Fourteen days after the vessel left Hobson's Bay, a dreadful storm arose. She pitched and laboured fearfully, the rudder was carried away, and she drifted helplessly before the wind. The seas made clean breaches over her. The masts went overboard with a terrific crash, killing several of the poor passengers who were clinging in desperation to the ropes and bulwarks, and soon after she struck heavily, close to some land which could be dimly seen looming ahead. Morning at length broke, and disclosed a smooth sandy beach about three hundred yards distant. The boats were got out, and with great difficulty and danger the remaining passengers and crew were safely landed. Sails were procured, and temporary shelter was provided for the women and children, some of whom were nearly naked, having rushed from their cabins with only such clothes as they happened to have on.

Fanny and Jack landed safely. When they found time to look about them, what was their horror and alarm to find that they had been cast ashore on a part of Balcke's run, and that they were not more than fifteen miles from the home-station! Their first impulse was to fly from the dangerous locality. There was no way of escape, however. They were starving, and had hardly enough clothes to cover themselves with. All their money was on board, and the vessel was full of water and breaking up fast.

Jack told the captain that he knew the country well, and he volunteered to go to the nearest station. He and some of the men went off to bring supplies. When they got near the place his courage completely failed. He pointed out the road, saying, at the same time, that he had sprained his knee, and could proceed no further. When they left him he dived into the depths of the forest, and walked and ran as fast as he could, his only anxiety being to get away, as far as possible, from the detestable spot.

Balcke sent down some bullock drays with liberal

supplies, and he accompanied them, in order to ren-
der any assistance in his power. He was astonished
to find Fanny crouched under some old sails. She
was overcome with shame. She confessed all, and
implored his forgiveness. He pitied her from his
heart, but turned away, and refused to hold any
further communication with her. Mr. Hardcliffe
was more hard-hearted, for when he arrived next
day he gave her in charge for conspiracy and at-
tempted murder. Jack was soon after captured.

They were tried, and pleaded guilty. Fanny
was sentenced to three years' imprisonment, and
Jack to fourteen years on the roads, the first three
in irons.

It remains but to add that Balcke was thus
able to explain everything to Miss Hardcliffe.
They were married soon afterwards, and they still
live beloved by all who know them.

ALL FOR GLITTERING GOLD

ALL FOR GLITTERING GOLD

IT was about the end of the year 185– when I reached Melbourne. I had been digging for a few weeks at Bendigo, in the old Eaglehawk Gully; and such a slice of luck as I had, I verily believe, never fell to the lot of any 'hatter,' for so we used to call a poor unfortunate fellow who had to work all by himself, without a mate to talk to or cheer him up when low. I should say, rather a good many slices of luck; for, had they all been put together, they would have well-nigh made a 'plum,' a 'pile,' a fortune, or anything else you choose to call it.

I had a deposit receipt sewn up in my belt for one thousand and three ounces two pennyweights of gold.

'A pretty round sum,' I says to the Gold Commissioner.

'Yes,' says he, in a joking way; 'round enough for you to take out a circular note with.'

'No, no,' says I. 'I'll have nothing to do with notes of any sort; for, what with forgeries and broken banks, a man is never safe unless he has the hard cash in his pocket.'

Well, as I have said, I had come from Bendigo; for I had made up my mind to go home as quickly as possible to Mary and the bairns, that I might give them a share of the comforts I could now afford. Poor things! they must have had a hard fight of it in the nine months I was away.

I thought, before I left them, that it was better to go away than to remain at home and starve, which I saw would be our fate sooner or later; so I put the few pounds I had remaining, after paying my passage, into Mary's hand, and, with tears in our eyes, we bade each other good-bye. Not in words; we were too far gone for that. Our hearts were too full. I could not bring myself to say good-bye to the bairns, so I kissed them all, more than a dozen times, as they lay asleep in their beds, little thinking that they wouldn't see me for a long, long time. I had never seen them looking so beautiful or innocent before, and the sight nearly made me change my mind, even after the passage money was paid, and my things on board the vessel. However, that

sorrowful time is over, and there is nothing but
happiness now; so I need not vex myself about our
past griefs.

I thought to myself, when I walked about the
Melbourne streets, what hobby-horses, and dolls,
and toys of one sort and another I would buy
when I got to London; how I would load myself
with cakes, and nuts, and sweeties, and gingerbread,
and get new dresses all round, and make Mary and
Tom, and Jack and Lily, as happy as the day was
long.

I began to look out for a ship, and used to walk
up and down, examining the large posters that were
stuck on the sheds and hoardings, down by the
wharves on the river Yarra. I noticed that the vessels
were all A1's, strong, staunch, and rapid sailers; so it
was a rather difficult thing to choose the best, when
they were all so good. Nearly every one of the
bills, too, had splendid woodcuts of a magnificent
ship in full sail, with every stitch of canvas set—a
perfect cloud of it, and not one in the sky; for they
would wish you to believe that each shipping company has fair weather bespoke for the run home,
and a choice of the kindest and most skilful captains;
the most abundant and expensive luxuries, making
the tables groan all day long; that there were no

such things as howling hurricanes, raging seas, smashed bulwarks, and leaking ships.

Another thing that struck me was, that none of the captains had ever made a voyage without having a testimonial, a purse of sovereigns, a gold cup, or a chronometer or two presented by the admiring passengers for the amiable qualities and skilful seamanship displayed on the voyage out. It's my belief that, when the subscribers awake some fine morning and find themselves gliding along under Cape Otway, or slipping up the coast off the Barwon Heads, or rattling through the ' Rip ' with the flood tide, they suddenly feel so overjoyed, because their voyage is so near the end, that they begin to look at each other with beaming faces, and in a few minutes forget all the miseries, troubles and quarrels they have had on the way. Then they call a meeting in the saloon, and have a glass or two of sherry or champagne. Then they feel a glow of delight at the prospect of getting ashore. Then they simmer a little—get a little warmer—then hot—and, at last, fairly boil over with brotherly love, which is usually all lavished on the captain (lucky dog !), in the shape of a purse, perhaps a hot-water jug or tea-urn, whereby they let off the steam, which has been worked up to high-pressure.

They have put down their names and sovereigns impulsively, and are precious sorry afterwards when they come to their senses.

The wharves looked dismal enough. It had been raining heavily for some days, and everything was thoroughly soaked. Piles of goods of all sorts lay about in the open air, without shelter. Tons and tons of flour appeared to be completely spoiled, and would never do its duty as bread, except in the shape of 'damper'—which admits of doubt, as it was as damp as it well could be. Sugar was wasting its sweetness through the gaping planks, and was sucked away by the eddying river. It was a melting sight to see the bags of salt quickly collapsing, and dissolving like snow in a mid-day thaw. Perishable and imperishable articles were alike uncared for, and everything was recklessly tumbled about in every possible position.

After thinking over the matter a good deal, I at last determined to go by a vessel that was advertised to sail in a few days. She was said to be a splendid ship of a thousand tons, and the agent told me, in confidence, that she was as fine a vessel as had ever entered the port, and that she was everything that a man of my sound judgment could wish for. Of course I had not seen her, for she was lying well out

in the bay, and the weather was too rough for me
to think of putting off to her. I did not, however,
quite believe what the agent said, and might have
made a slight inquiry; but when he spoke of my
sound judgment it rather mastered me, I must ·
confess, for I prided myself on seeing as far as most
folks, and, of course, was just as liable to give way
to flattery.

Well, I paid my passage money, and was told
to be on board the next day; but, on going down
to the office I found that the sailing of my ship was
postponed for a week, owing to rough weather. At
the end of the week there was another delay for
want of sailors, most of the crew having run away.
Then one thing and another intervened, causing
more time to be wasted, until I was completely tired
and disgusted, and had well nigh thrown up all
idea of going in her, when one morning I learned,
to my intense satisfaction, that the passengers and
gold were to be on board the steamer, at Cole's
Wharf, by two o'clock.

I had noticed that wherever I went about the
wharves I saw a tall, Yankee-looking fellow. He
never seemed to look at me, but he appeared to
dodge my footsteps and stealthily watch my movements. I could not help feeling a sort of indefin-

able dread of the man, and sometimes I endeavoured
to give him the slip by darting up a right of-way,
or getting into a crowd. He was, however, always
too quick for me. When I thought I had got away
unobserved, I soon found that he was shuffling close
behind me looking quite unconcerned. Just after
I had learned at the shipping office that I was to be
on board the steamer by two o'clock, and was turning away from the clerk, I found that my tall friend
was close beside me, and, I expect, had heard every
word of the conversation.

As I was obliged to go to the Treasury with my
receipt in order to draw the gold, I hired a drayman
to take my trunk and carpet-bag, which was all the
luggage I meant to take. The trunk was full of
warm serviceable clothing; the bag contained only
a few shavings and old papers. I pretended that
the bag was very heavy, and got quite red in the
face lifting it into the dray. I was going to put the
gold into it, and it would never have done to show
the drayman that I was taking an empty bag into
the Gold Office light as a feather, and bringing it
out with a full load of nothing but gold.

When we reached the place, I got off the dray
and told the man that I was going in to get a few
ounces of gold which a good friend of mine had

sent me. Of course, I was the friend, and the best friend I had too.

After getting inside the office I ran back to the dray and took up the carpet-bag, saying at the same time that I had forgotten the deposit receipt that was in it, and that I would take it with me into the office. I then lifted it down, and put as much apparent strength into the movement as I supposed my one thousand and three ounces would require if I were carrying them.

I was not long in producing the receipt. The gold was shoved over the counter, and I bundled it into the bag in double quick time, and was outside in a minute or two; but before I'd got to the dray my shirt was as wet as if I'd lain in a water-hole all night, and my face was beaded over with perspiration like a red cabbage covered with dew-drops on a spring morning. It took all the strength I was master of, and all the breath I wasn't master of, for I was completely knocked out of time, in getting the confounded bag into the dray; and right glad I was when it was done.

' You've got a pretty stiff load, mate,' said the drayman.

' Yes,' said I, ' on my mind.'

' How's that ? ' said he.

'Well, I did not get such good news inside as I expected, and it has made me a little faint like. If you'd believe me, I could hardly carry that bag back again, I felt so queer.'

'Nonsense! the bag isn't so light as you gammon it is, mate. Let *me* try its weight.'

This put me on my mettle in more ways than one, for I sat down on the gold to keep him from lifting it, and swore at him heavily, telling him he was a lazy rascal for keeping me all day, when I ought to be on board the steamer.

'Look here, mate,' says he, 'I'm blowed if you'll bounce *me*, or make *me* believe that bag has anything but bricks and old iron in it, which you're trotting about pretending it's luggage. Look here, my lad, have you paid your board and lodging, and your laundress, if you ever had one? And who are you going to take in next? I'm blest if I don't raise the shafts and tip you out in the mud, bricks and old iron and all.'

'My good man,' reasoned I, 'I did not mean to offend you. If you take me to the steamer as quickly as you can, I'll give you a pound.'

'I'm blest if I move under a fiver after such insultin' language from a chap who's skulking home because he's too lazy to work.'

E

'The man's mad or drunk. If I am compelled by misfortune to go home, is it likely, do you think, that I am so flush of money as to have a five-pound note to throw away?'

'Here goes then. If you don't tip *me*, I'll tip *you* and your precious stones into the gutter.'

He got down from the dray and loosened the harness, and was just about to carry his threat into execution, when I saw the affair was becoming serious, and that the rascal really meant to tip me. I gave one hasty glance up and down the street, in the hazy hope that there might be a policeman in sight, but you might then as well have looked for a needle on Keilor Plains as for one of those guardians of the peace when you happened to want him. Of course I could not see one.

Just at this moment the tall Yankee I had seen so often came hulking past. He looked steadily at me for a moment or so, and then walked quickly away.

'Is it a bargain, then?' said the drayman. 'Say the word, and it's all right; if you don't, it's all wrong.'

'Well, I give in. You'll get the fiver if you make haste. I hear the steamer's bell. There is not a moment to lose. Jump up.'

By this time he had got the harness all right, and he jumped upon the dray. We rattled down the street at a tremendous rate, dashing through the cross gutters and in and out of the mud-holes in anything but a pleasant manner. In a few minutes we were alongside Cole's Wharf. I jumped down and rushed on board the steamer, as I saw there was no time to lose. The excitement seemed to give me strength; I was astonished at the ease with which I got the bag on board. I ran back for the trunk, and had just got my foot on the vessel, when she moved off. My friend the drayman was evidently moved too, for he began to yell at the top of his voice:

'Where's the fiver? Throw us the fiver Make haste with ye?'

I had an inclination to pay him out by not paying him at all; but on second thoughts I took a pound note from my pocket, and, as I had said I would give him a fiver, I wrapped up a five-shilling piece—a different fiver from that which he expected to receive—in the note, and threw it, with all my strength, straight towards him. It hit him with considerable force on the right eye. He dropped his whip, and threw up his hands, as if in pain.

The steamer was now under way, and began to go at full speed. I saw my questionable friend, the drayman, for the last time, when we were turning a bend of the river. He was straining to look at me, while he raised his arm in impotent rage and shook it at me, yelling at the same time that he would do for me if he ever caught me ashore.

The banks of the river were very dirty. Disgusting-looking pigs were wandering among heaps of garbage and gorging on offal. Sheepskins and bullock hides, fresh from the beasts, were spread out on grimy fences, and reeking in the fetid air. Heaps of dirty wool lay ready for the fellmongers. Pyramids of bones, hideous, ghastly, and foul, were piled about in every place. Bullocks roaring with pain and thirst stood in small yards, firmly fixed in the thick black mud. Sight and smell were alike offended, and there was a general holding of noses at almost every turn of the river, as some new abomination was blown towards us.

We soon got out of this neighbourhood, however, and steamed along between the tall scrub that fringed the banks. Here we could breathe and look around with some degree of comfort. A

fleet of lighters was coming up, laden to the
water's edge with merchandise of all kinds and
from every clime. The goods were soaking wet
from the heavy showers that scudded over us.
The great round clouds were rolling up, full of
threatening rain, growing blacker the more they
poured. We had no shelter, and in a minute or
two we were all in utter misery. We were not
only wet, but chilled to the bone with the sharply
cutting breeze.

When we arrived at the mouth of the river the
steamer began to tumble about and the decks were
washed at every lurch. I began to think of my gold
and what I should do to avoid notice. The best
thing to be done, I thought, was to turn out some
of my clothes from the trunk, and do them up in a
bundle, so as to make room for my carpet bag,
which I did. I then locked and strapped my trunk,
and imagined I had done a wise thing. I had just
got all snug when we arrived at the vessel, the
'Mary Jane,' Captain Googe, commander.

I got my trunk and bundle on board without
much difficulty, and had them removed at once to
my cabin. I was a rich man now, and had, therefore, taken a berth in the saloon. I meant to enjoy
myself as much as I could, as a sort of compen-

sation for the voyage out, and I had spared neither time nor money in making things meet my views.

As the day wore on the weather improved. At sunset the clouds had nearly all disappeared. There was a full moon and the stars shone brightly. The wind had fallen; there was a calm, peaceful flood of light gilding the waters, and the shores of the bay were almost lost in the dreamy haze that shut in the view.

I dressed myself in a good suit of broadcloth, and, as I gave the few last touches to my toilet, I flattered myself that I looked like a man of means, and a decent unit of society. When I was living cheaply and even meanly in Melbourne—for I had my secret to keep—I did not seem to realise that I was the possessor of so much wealth, but now I could indulge a little after so much self-sacrifice. I sometimes think that the pleasure of wealth consists, to some extent, in the opinion people have of its possessor. Had the captain seen me a short time previously, he would certainly not have noticed me. Now he stopped and shook hands and hoped I would enjoy the trip.

When the bell rang for tea I went into the saloon and took my seat near the foot of the table. From this position, I had a good opportunity of seeing my fellow-passengers, and I scanned their faces with some interest. There were only ten of us in all. I afterwards learnt that there were none in the steerage or second cabin. On the captain's right sat a German lady, Mrs. Schniedelhause, and on the left Mr. Schniedelhause. He was a dealer in jewellery, and was going to his own country for a few months to pick up bargains for export to Victoria.

His wife was a confirmed invalid, constantly grumbling and boring everyone with her bodily complaints. As soon as she had taken her seat she said to the captain, 'Mine head is like to shplit. It ish de vetter, or de shmell of de ship's inside.'

Just at that moment, a tall figure came stooping in, and took his seat next Mr. Schniedelhause. Think of my astonishment and alarm when I recognised the Yankee who had so often dogged my footsteps. There was no mistake about it. There he sat, and I could not help thinking that I had never seen a more villanous-looking fellow. He was not heavy, apparently, but muscular and strong, with broad shoulders and a capacious chest, and he always carried a brace of pistols stuck in his belt, which gave him a ferocious look.

He soon informed us, addressing us all round,

that his name was Abel Wincoop, a citizen of the U-nited States, and that he was death on niggers, a crack shot, and didn't care a cuss for creation.

A gloomy, taciturn man sat next him, who turned out to be an intimate friend of Abel's. I do not think he was an American, although he always professed to be one. He was more like an Irishman, I thought, and his name being Mulligan was some support to my idea.

The other passengers were, a quiet, respectable ironmonger of the name of Jones, Captain Bravery, of the Queen's Own, and a widow lady, Mrs. Smith, with her two little girls.

The ship's captain was a fine specimen of the British sailor of the old school. He was slow but sure, strict with his men, and inclined to carry matters with a high hand—at least I thought he was a little too severe sometimes.

Of course we were all rather reserved at first, and our conversation, like a broken-down fence, had a good many gaps in it. The Yankee did most of the talking, which, however, was not addressed to anyone in particular, but seemed to be meant for the lamp, or the barometer that hung over the table.

I soon turned in for the night, and immediately fell asleep. I was dreaming away until daylight about Yankees, revolvers, and bowie-knives. It was a sort of continuous half-sleep, the effect of unpleasant day-thoughts. Next morning the gold arrived on board. There were nearly a hundred thousand ounces in all, packed in small wooden boxes. These boxes were carefully guarded by some of the bank officials, who saw them securely stowed away in the ship's safe.

We were now only awaiting the arrival of the able-bodied seamen who had run away from the ship when she came into port, but who were soon captured and lodged in gaol for safe keeping until the vessel would be ready for sea. In a few minutes we saw the boat belonging to the water police making towards us with the men on board. As the fellows clambered up one by one, they looked as sullen and hang-dog a set as ever I had seen.

In half an hour we were under way, and spanking down the bay at the rate of eight knots an hour. The very sight of the sea always has an exhilarating effect on me; I felt like a schoolboy going home for the holidays; and it set the blood dancing through my veins to think of the pleasures in store for me, for I should soon see dear old England again, and clasp my darlings, Mary, and Tom, and Jack, and Lily, to my heart once more. How the little things will have grown! I thought. Why, ten to one, I shan't know them at the first glance, and they will almost have forgotten me.

On we went, past St. Kilda, Brighton, Frankston, and Schnapper Point. The wind was increasing, and the waves were skipping up the ship's sides as if curious to see what sort of people there were on board. On they came, larger and larger, now breaking on our bows and showering the decks for many a yard, now thumping broadside on with a dull thud, and then lifting the ship on their great backs and giving us a shove on our way.

The sea is the champagne of water; sparkling, beading, effervescent, bright, and clear. It quickens the pulse, exhilarating the whole man into a never-failing feeling of delight. I thought myself the happiest fellow alive, for I had not a care. Every hour would take me nearer home, and that was pleasure in itself.

We were outside the heads by dusk, and went dashing away eastward. The long coast-line faded into amethyst, and was lost in the distance. The hills loomed up grim and dark, and looked like immense lumps of indigo. A few faint streaks of light still lingered in the western sky; and soon, night, black night, drew around us, and shut out all but the clouds and stars.

Nothing occurred worth relating during the first fortnight. The weather was fine, and we made a first-rate run. We were very comfortable in every way, excepting that Abel Wincoop and his friend Mulligan made themselves rather disagreeable now and then. I, however, kept out of their way, and did not mix myself in any disputes that they got into with the other passengers. They endeavoured to do their utmost in order to make me quarrel with them, but I quietly got away as quickly as I could and so avoided open warfare.

One evening we were sitting at tea. The conversation was a little more lively and pleasant than usual, and I began to think we might enjoy ourselves pretty well in spite of the little peculiarities of Abel and Mulligan. Pompey, the black steward, seemed to have an instinctive dread of the Yankee, and shunned him as much as possible. On this especial evening Pompey kept as far from him as he could. Abel saw this, and took every opportunity of calling for something or other, in order to make Pompey come round the table to assist him.

'You darned nigger, I guess I'll take a cake,' said Abel.

'Yes, massa.'

'I want a cake for an answer, not the everlastin' "Yes, massa." Look spry, will ye!'

Poor Pompey turned pale with fright, and stammered :

'Yes, massa. Coming, massa.'

He then shuffled round the table with a plate of cakes, and stopped behind Abel to offer them. The Yankee deliberately turned round, rolled an enormous quid of tobacco in his mouth which he had kept there all the time he was eating, and expectorated straight in Pompey's face. The tobacco-juice trickled down the poor negro's cheeks, and made him look more pitiable than before.

'Mr. Wincoop,' said the captain, 'I am both astonished and grieved. I beg of you to observe at least a decent behaviour when at this table, and, what is more, I shall insist upon it.'

'I du declare, 'twould rile a sucking pig,' said Abel, addressing the barometer, 'tu hear old Googe coming the *hu*-mane so precipitous, and all along of that darned nigger. Why, look here; I just spit in the only dirty place I could find handy, and if that ain't decent, why, I'd better go to school again for another quarter.'

Pompey stood grinding his teeth until Abel had

finished speaking, and then he burst out in a roar.

'Ha, ha! I know you. Do you hear? I know you. You're not my massa. De cap'en is my massa, and berry kind too.'

'That will do, Pomp. Go to your pantry,' said the captain.

'No, massa! Not till I've exposed dat black teffel of a villain—dat tief—dat rascal—dat scoun-drel.' (Pompey had prefixed strong adjectives, and now began to gesticulate and dance like a madman.) 'Dat murderer!' (Adjective again.) Dat's Yankee Thunder, the bushranger. I know him—I know him! Here's his picter. Look at him!'

He pulled out a portrait from his pocket, and held it up so that we could all see it. Sure enough, there was Abel Wincoop to the life—every feature, and his very expression.

Pompey had barely time to show it before Abel pulled out his bowie-knife. A bright glitter shot through the air, and Pompey fell, screaming wildly.

We were horror-struck for a moment, and then all was confusion and uproar. I ran to Pompey and raised him up. Some one dashed a cup of tea in his face, and, with this reviver, he opened his eyes and rolled them wildly. Abel's knife had struck him in the fleshy part of the arm, and was still sticking there. I pulled it out gently and then tore open his shirt and looked at the wound, which I at once saw was a very simple one and would be easily cured.

Pompey thought he was a dead man and refused to move, so two of us carried him to his bunk, and rolled him in and left him to come to at his leisure.

When I went back to the saloon Abel and Mulligan were gone. We were all as silent as if a thunderbolt had fallen. among us. Here was a subject for wonder, and a sensation in our quiet community of quite an unexpected kind. I took up a book and vainly tried to read. Then I took a pack of cards and endeavoured to play, first double dummy, and then patience, but I could not keep my thoughts on the game for a moment. At last I went out and walked on deck, and for a long time leant over the bulwarks dreamily watching the waves as they bubbled and hissed away behind.

I began to cogitate on the incident of the evening, and could not help connecting with it Abel's suspicious movements in following me about the streets of Melbourne. I began to fear that he must have ascertained, in some way, that

I had so much gold, and was only waiting his opportunity to get rid of me and secure it for himself. Pompey had thrown a new light on my former speculations regarding the Yankee, which filled me with new fear. On board ship, however, I was safe enough; I would be on my guard. To be forewarned was to be forearmed, so I looked out my revolver, and from that evening I carried it in the breast pocket of my coat.

I had not been many minutes on deck when I heard little Jenny Smith laughing heartily with a childish, silvery laugh. I was very fond of the child, so I went towards the sound. To my astonishment I saw Abel with Jenny on his shoulder. He was capering and dancing, and making fun for her. His cadaverous face was actually lit up with pleasure, and —I could not deny it, although I had taken a violent antipathy to the man—there was even a good expression on it.

'You are a naughty boy, so you must go in the corner,' said Jenny.

'Don't be angry, don't, or I'll cry,' said Abel.

'Yes, I will; let me down.'

'Kiss me then.'

She stooped down and kissed his leathern jaws as if she loved him, and patted his great ugly head as tenderly as if he had been her own father. He lifted her down gently, and set her on her feet.

'Now, sir, if you are naughty still, you must go in the corner, and you will get no supper.'

'Boo hoo hoo, I will be good, indeed I will, and never be a bad boy any more.'

I could hardly believe my eyes and ears. Here was a man I believed to be a thoroughpaced villain—a murderer in fact—if what Pompey said was true, for it was well known that Yankee Thunder, if indeed it was he, was one of the most bloodthirsty scoundrels alive. He could not be the man! It was impossible that a double-dyed scoundrel could thus gambol with a child and be loved by her. Surely little Jenny would have instinctively shunned him—would have been re- pelled from him—had he been the man I was beginning to suspect him to be.

I passed on without speaking, and lay down upon some sails that had been laid on the top of the fo'castle. I tried to banish the Yankee from my mind, but could not. He was always stum- bling across my path and casting gloomy shadows into my heart. He was poisoning my very existence, and making me miserable. I wished a thousand times that I had disposed of my gold, and that I had remitted the amount through the Bank of England.

I must have fallen asleep, I think, for when I awoke the moon was well up in the sky. I had no sooner ascertained this than a great jagged cloud went raking across her face, and blotted her out. A black wall was packed up on the horizon, which was rapidly broken up by the rising storm, and hurled overhead in inky masses. The wind was whistling through the rigging and snapping the ropes like whips.

I was about to jump on the deck, when some voices just below me, at the fo'castle door, caught my ears. I did not want to disturb the speakers, so I thought I would lie a moment longer. I could not help hearing the first sentence, and had no alternative but to remain until the close of the conversation.

A voice that seemed familiar said, 'The old man could be knocked on the head, you know, and the old tub could be scuttled, and there's an end to the whole affair.'

'I'll pay him out, shiver his timbers! He struck me once, and the mark has burnt into my cheek with rage and hate.'

'The passengers will stand by you like old

F

Hickory, and lend a hand like a greased streak of lightning. There's the gold, too. Why, man, we might all retire from business and set up in the grand milor style, Señor this, and Hidalgo that, in Texas or Mexico.'

' I'm your man, never fear.'

I heard some footsteps coming. The voices ceased. I distinctly saw Abel's friend, Mulligan, wriggling away among the barrels and empty hencoops, and his companion, one of the sailors, at the same time slunk into the fo'castle.

' Reef the mainsail,' shouted the captain from the poop.

' Aye, aye, sir.'

The storm would soon be upon us, and the sailors were busy making preparations for it. I crept away to my cabin, fully determined to warn the captain of the dangerous characters he had on board.

The rushing sounds of the wind were now fierce and strong, and I had hardly reached the saloon before the ship heeled over on one side, and dashed madly through the water. The hurry and noise on deck gradually ceased, and everyone seemed anxiously to wait for the full force of the storm. We all knew this was but the feeble buffeting of the gale, to what we had yet to pass through. The wind increased every second, until it raved and howled around us in all its fury. Nothing was now heard but the crack of the ropes, the whistling of the gale in the rigging, and the dash of the foam that flew from our bows like the spray from a cataract.

After an age, as it seemed to me, I heard the captain shout, 'Double-reef the topsails.'

There was no answer to this order, apparently, for he shouted louder than before,

'Double-reef topsails, do you hear? Mr. Gaunt, where are your men?'

'Aye, aye, sir,' said Mr. Gaunt.

In another minute the captain rushed into his cabin, and dashed out again with a brace of pistols in his hands. There was a loud trampling, and a volley of oaths and threats; then the captain was heard again.

'I'll shoot the first man who refuses. Up you go, or you'll all be in Davy Jones's locker in five minutes.'

During this time the wind was still increasing, and the sea was rising higher and higher. Huge rollers rose like mountains over the stern, and were mown as if with some giant scythe, and dashed over us in a blinding deluge. The white surges leaped up above the heavy seas, and the air was full of hissing, glittering spray. The vessel yielded more and more to the storm, and, in less than an hour from the time we were struck, she was driving along with tremendous force, while the gale raged around us with awful fury.

We had a terrible time of it. Women were praying and screaming, children were crying, and men were holding their breath with fear, while their faces were white with terror. I thought it was all over with us, so I commended Mary and the bairns to God, and silently prayed that He might have mercy on myself. Our prayers were heard, for, just as we imagined our end had come, the wind began to blow less fiercely. The gale was spent, and we breathed more freely and felt we were saved.

No one lay down all night. When the first streaks of dawn began to show I turned in and soon fell asleep. When I awoke the sun was shining brightly, and the vessel was moving along in a comfortable way. I peeped out of my porthole, and saw that the sea had gone down in a most surprising manner.

The morning was as fine a one as I could wish

to see. The sky was of a deep blue, and the few feathery flakes that dappled it floated lazily, as if making up for their wild orgy of the night before.

I had forgotten to wind up my watch, so it had run down, but I guessed that the time might be about ten o'clock. I was not far wrong, for I soon heard five bells strike. I wound up my watch and set it accordingly. After I had dressed, I turned the handle of my cabin door. It was stiff, so I shook it smartly as it would not turn. After trying to get out for some time. I got quite cross and rattled the door and kicked it with some force, but all to no purpose.

'Keep quiet there, will you?' said a gruff voice on the other side, 'or I'll put a bullet through you.'

I distinctly heard a trigger click, which was an argument not to be gainsaid; so I kept quiet as I was told, thinking it the safest course to pursue, as I was caged like a mouse in a trap.

'You're a dead man if you make a sound,' said the voice again, in a tone which chilled me to the bone, for I recognised it as Mulligan's, the arch-villain I had overheard the night before plotting with one of the men.

Just at that moment footsteps passed overhead, and then others followed with a cat-like tread. My senses seemed preternaturally acute, and I verily believe I could have heard a man's heart beat at twenty paces. Mine thumped so loudly that I almost expected Mulligan would put a bullet through me for making a noise.

There was a blow struck, and a heavy body fell on deck. Then there was a suppressed groan, a quick movement of naked feet, and all was still for a few minutes. Then a number of men entered the cabin. I knew that Abel was at their head by his shambling gait, and from his habit of rubbing against the cabin doors with his shoulders as he slouched in. He stopped opposite the captain's cabin, and put his eye to the keyhole. Although I could not see him, I knew instinctively every movement. After a patient scrutiny he undid some fastenings on the outside, turned the handle stealthily, and swung the door wide open. Then he dashed at the captain, who was lying asleep in his bunk, tired out with the previous night's exertions. The movement awoke him, and he tried to rise, but Abel was too quick for him, for he seized him by the arms with an iron grasp.

The captain was a powerful man, and struggled for a moment or two. With a sudden spring he managed to throw himself on the Yankee's shoulders, and got one arm free. He then clutched Abel by the throat, and tried to strangle him; but he, seeing his danger, heaved his antagonist against the beams overhead with fearful violence. There was an awful crash, and the contest was over. The apparently lifeless body of the captain was then tossed into the bunk. The Yankee staggered back a step or two, and fell in a swoon.

The hand-to-hand fight I have just described did not last two minutes. When it began I dashed headlong at the door and tried to burst it open, but it was too strong, and I made no impression on the stout timbers, which only seemed to mock my puny efforts.

'Oh, goot shentlemens! prave mens, don't plow my prains out. T'ey are pad enough already, for mine head is like to shplit,' screamed poor Mrs. Schniedelhause from her cabin, where it seems she was shut up.

'Hold your tongue, you she cat,' roared Mulligan.

'Oh, kind Americans! here ish two thalers, a sixpence, a fourpence piece, my vatch and key, which are all gold, shentlemens, I assure you, and not prass as Mrs. Marks said, but it vas only envy, and no more, and she did not pelieve it herself. And here ish a prooch and my earrings. All dese

tings I will you give, if you vill not kill me. Oh !
mine head is like to shplit.'

'Where is your better half?' said Mulligan,
opening her door.

'Mine vorser half you mean. He ish unter de
bunks. Oh, you scoundrels!'—shaking her fist
under the berth—'I vill make you suffer for pring-
ing me here to be plown out of prains, and shut up
in my cabins and murdered.'

'Come out, Snivelcrawler,' said Mulligan, giving
him a kick on the shins, and dragging him out.
'We have nothing to say to women and cowards
like you.'

'Oh, mine goot Mishter Mulligan, ish it you?
You have avake me out of a shound shleep, to have
de pleasure of seeing you the first times I avake.
Vat vill you have to trink, mine noble sirs ? It ish
cold, for mine teeth is shattering.'

'Wall, I feel poorly; I feel poorly. A leetle
tightness in the chest. If you have any loose gold
pieces knocking around, they're a sovereign remedy
—a sovereign remedy, do you hear?—for my com-
plaint.'

'You vill have your jokes, Mishter Mulligan.
Oh ! you are a funnee fellow, Mishter Mulligan.'

Mulligan stepped behind him, and pinioned his

arms. Schniedelhause did not resist, except in mild protest, for he was half dead with fright.

I now heard the voice of Jones the ironmonger, muttering curses on Abel and Mulligan, which if not loud were certainly deep.

I afterwards heard that he had knocked Mulligan down, and had given Abel some trouble before he was secured. He always seemed a very meek little man, so I am sure the mutineers were rather astonished at the resistance he made.

Captain Bravery, I also found out, was the first man captured. They pounced upon him while asleep, and they immediately gagged him to keep him from raising an alarm.

The mutineers had now secured the captain and mates—who were knocked down on deck—and all the male passengers except myself.

By this time most of the crew were quite tipsy, having taken advantage of the row to break into the spirit-room. Abel, Mulligan, and a few of the ringleaders, were, however, perfectly sober, and were endeavouring to keep order.

I soon heard the Yankee's shuffling steps coming my way. He stopped at my door, and told me, after he had unfastened it, that I could walk out, which I did with a loaded pistol in each hand.

If any personal violence had been offered me at that moment, I should certainly have shot the first person who meddled with me. No one spoke to me, or interfered with me. I looked round and found Captain Bravery, Jones, and Schniedelhause sitting in a corner, in a very woebegone state.

'You had better put down your pistols, old hoss,' said Abel, 'for if you don't, them boys,' pointing to the skylight through which the muzzles of four guns were pointed full at me, 'will make crow's meat of you in another second.'

I gave one earnest glance all round. Every way of escape was barred against me. Abel had a cutlass and pistols lying on the table before him. Mulligan stood at the other end of the saloon with a rifle pointed at me. The odds were fearfully against me. I threw my weapons behind me, and stepped towards Abel, for with all his faults I preferred giving myself up to him, rather than to Mulligan, whom I utterly abhorred.

'Bind him,' said Abel.

Two men seized me from behind, and dexterously tied me hand and foot with stout ropes. They then unceremoniously gave me a push, and I tumbled into the corner beside my fellow sufferers.

All this time poor Mrs. Smith was shut up in

her cabin, and half dead with fright. Her little girls, who could hardly have comprehended the full state of the case, were crying like to break their hearts; while their mother was sobbing convulsively, and occasionally going off into hysterics.

The conspirators were in complete possession of the ship, and were strutting about with the greatest assurance possible. The Yankee had taken command, and gave orders to alter the ship's course. I saw him through the skylight, coolly taking an observation of the sun. In a few minutes he came into the saloon, with the quadrant stuck jauntily under his arm, and sat down at the table to work out the calculations. He was not long in doing them, and I felt certain, from his business-like manner, that he was quite at home in the work. This idea was confirmed when he pricked off the ship's position on the chart. Our position, I was about to write, but *we* were woefully out in *our* reckoning.

The captain had been completely stunned, and seemed, from what I heard, to be dead, but now began to show signs of reviving. By the aid of some stimulants which Pompey was ordered to pour down his throat, he was soon restored. He began to storm and rave like a madman, and threatened and coaxed by turns; but, as no one heeded him, he ceased after about an hour's violent use of his lungs.

It was well on in the afternoon when Abel shouted, 'Clear away the long boat.'

This order was quickly obeyed, for we soon heard the ropes passing through the blocks.

'Pass out the prisoners—Googe first, and gag him.'

Mulligan gagged the captain in spite of his vigorous protests, and four sailors carried him out, notwithstanding his determined attempts at resistance.

Captain Bravery was carried out next, complaining of the indignity put upon an officer and a gentleman. Jones's turn came next; then Mrs. Schniedelhause was bundled out, declaring, as usual, that 'her head was like to shplit.' Her husband was taken next, and then I was carried out like the others. I was hoisted over the ship's side, and lowered into the boat, which was swinging about a foot from the water. I found my companions in trouble all huddled together, and looking the very picture of distress.

Mrs. Smith was now brought out, with her little girls, who had stopped crying.

'Ma'am,' said Abel, 'if you'll sail with us, you'll be as slick and comfortable as we can make you; and as for the little girls, why they'll have no end of kindness, for *they* never shunned me, and *they* never hated me like all the rest of them cusses in the boat. If it had not been for your girls, and their innocent ways, where do you think you'd all be now? Why, nowhere—in Davy Jones's locker, which tells no tales. That's where you'd be, every mother's son of you. I've played with them, Mrs. Smith, and wished I was a boy again, playing under the maple trees at my old home. I've wished I'd been took when a youngster.' Here he dashed his hand across his eyes. 'But that's neither here nor there now.'

I felt sure he wiped a tear from his eye.

'What's the use of preachin'?' said Mulligan; 'bundle over, you brats.'

Little Jenny began to cry, and clung to Abel's knees.

'Darn it!' roared Abel, 'you've raised my dander. The very infants know you're a devil incarnate. But you'll swing for it, if your foul tongue offends them again.'

'Don't let him kill me,' said Jenny, addressing Abel.

'No, my pet, he shan't harm a hair of your head; and, what's more, no harm shall be done to any of you, big or little, for your sakes.' 'Wall, ma'am,' he added, 'will you sail with us or not? I'll land you safe and sound anywhere you like.'

'No, no,' said Mrs. Smith sobbing. 'I'll go with the others.'

'Very well, ma'am, I'll just go into the saloon, and bring out some blankets and warm things for you and the girls.'

He came back in a few minutes with Mrs. Smith's luggage, and a heap of blankets, which he lowered into the boat. He also threw in some mattresses, biscuits, preserved meats, and other stores; also a compass, quadrant, and chronometer. He then helped Mrs. Smith into the boat, also the little girls, after having kissed them.

Pompey had scrambled down unobserved, and was crouching behind the captain. Abel's sharp eyes soon detected him, and his manner altered in a moment.

'Come out of that, you darned nigger! You infernal cuss! make tracks or I'll shoot you dead.'

'Let me go, massa. Let me go, Mass Wincoop,' said Pompey, very piteously.

' No,' roared Abel, pointing his pistol at him.

' I'm comin', massa, comin'.'

Pompey, as he passed the captain, whispered something in his ear, which sent a ray of pleasure across his dejected face.

Pompey had no sooner reached the deck than he tried to dodge the blow that Abel aimed at him, but he could not avoid it, and he was sent sprawling on his back, making a terrific uproar as he half slid and half tumbled out of the way of the Yankee.

' Mrs. Smith,' said Abel, putting his head over the bulwarks, ' here's a knife. When the boat's adrift you can cut the cords and set everybody free. Lower away.'

' Aye, aye, sir,' said the men.

The boat touched the water, and floated quietly astern. We were fairly launched on the wide Pacific, which would, for aught we could see, soon be our grave.

After a few minutes Mrs. Smith cut the cords, and we were all free.

The sun was just setting. His great round face hung on the water, and burned with a dull red glare, lighting up the ship with splashes of crimson, from keel to top-mast. We seemed to be floating on a sea of blood, and all within our ken had a weird and ominous look, which chilled and awed me.

The captain was every inch a brave man. He took command of the boat, and issued his orders with as much coolness and decision as if he had been on board the 'Mary Jane.'

Captain Bravery, Jones, Schniedelhause, and I were ordered to take the oars, which we cheerfully did. The captain steered, and we were soon hard at work.

'Now, gentlemen,' said the captain, 'I am going to steer straight for my ship. As there is almost a calm, and as she has hardly any sail set, we ought to catch her up in a few hours' time. I count on your assistance. When I tell you that our lives depend on the coolness and courage you display, I need hardly urge you to do your very best. Only obey my instructions implicitly, and I do not doubt that all will be well with us soon.'

We all promised to carry out his orders to the very letter. Without knowing more of his plans, we prepared to do what we were told. His manner inspired us with confidence, and we worked with a will.

After a hard hour's rowing we lost sight of the ship altogether. The night was very dark, a thin veil of clouds having shut out the stars. We toiled on as well as we were able. The perspiration streamed from every pore. Being all landsmen, we did not handle our oars in the most approved fashion; still, we got on wonderfully well.

'Hurrah!' shouted the captain. 'I see her. Pompey has hung out a light. Look! there it is, straight ahead.'

There it was, sure enough, and a very bright light too. Our hopes, which had sunk to a very low ebb, began to rise again, and we all pulled with renewed vigour; the captain all the while encouraging us by his approval, and reporting from time to time that we were gaining on the ship.

'I'll bet you a pound,' said the captain, 'they haven't a man at the wheel, or he is drunk. She's boxing the compass, and no mistake, and yawing about in the most absurd way, just as if she had swallowed a hogshead of rum.'

It was near eleven o'clock, as we judged, when Captain George reported that we were within a quarter of a mile of the chase.

'Every man muffle his oar with a blanket,' said he.

This was soon done, and we went on our way

G

noiselessly. In half an hour more we were under the Mary Jane's stern.

The captain groped about, and at last found a rope dangling, to which we made fast, much to our relief, for we were beginning to feel rather tired.

Only some indistinct sounds were heard on board the ship. We were unable to say for some time what they were, but by patient listening we made out that three or four people were trying to sing a chorus, and were too drunk to come within twenty miles of the tune. Another group appeared to be quarrelling, in the last stages of helpless imbecility. Every sound spelt rum.

As we were all sitting as still as the grave, we were startled by seeing some dark object moving above us. We watched in breathless anxiety. Presently we saw a man peering all round, as if in search of something on the water. The captain closely scanned the man's movements for a short ime, and then whispered:

'Is that you, Pompey?'

'Yes, massa. Oh! I'se joyful to see you.'

I was sure he could not see anything of us, for he immediately said:

'Where are you, massa?'

'Here we are, just below you. Come down and tell us the news.'

'I'll be dar in a moment, cap'en, as de t'under said to de lightnin'.'

He went away for a moment, but soon came back and slid down the rope.

'Well, Pomp, what's our chance?'

'No chance at all, massa. Pomp doesn't leave it to chances. Sartain sure, an' no mistake! De fellars all as drunk as hogs. I fill 'em all up to de bunghole wid rum. It's de bully liquor, cap'en. De tam Yankee lock up de spirit-room for his own cheek, and put key in pocket; but dis chile warn't born yesterday. No, no! got 'nother key in Pompey's pocket, ya! ya! an' got power o' rum into fo'castle. Make all drunk as blazes.'

'Could you get us some pistols and cutlasses, Pompey?'

'All right, cap'en. Pompey all dar on 'casion like dis. Debbil of a cunning fellow is Pomp, massa. Come all up dis here rope an' you'll see.'

We all scrambled up, leaving the women and children in the boat, with strict injunctions not to move or make the slightest noise.

When we got on deck Pompey put a revolver

G 2

into each man's hand. We were also supplied with
a cutlass apiece.

We took off our boots, and crept round to the
saloon door and looked in. Abel and Mulligan
were at the head of the table, and appeared to be
very tipsy. Sam White and Ben Shakle, two of
the seamen and chief conspirators, were sitting near
them. They seemed helplessly drunk, and were
leaning on the table as if half asleep. Heaps
of sovereigns and gold-dust were piled up and
scattered about the table. The scoundrels had
evidently been dividing the plunder. The sight
of my carpet bag under Abel's elbow nearly drove
me mad, and I longed to put a bullet through him.
Was it for this that he had dogged me through the
streets of Melbourne? I vowed, there and then,
that I would be even with him yet.

Pompey came up, puffing and blowing, carrying
two buckets full of hot water, which sent up clouds
of steam.

'Wait a moment, massa; wait a moment till I
come back.'

He mounted the steps leading to the poop, and
went to one of the skylights which happened to be
just above Abel and Mulligan. He had no sooner
reached it than we were all startled by a loud noise

of falling water, and then screams of agony from the Yankee and his friend. The saloon was filled with steam in a moment, and we could not see what had occurred. Mingled with the screams we could hear Pompey shouting and laughing as loud as he could roar.

'Oh, golly! what a go! Ha, ha, ha! De debbils is in a hot place. Ha, ha, ha! Dat's hot liquor, Yankee Abel! Ho, ho, ho! Ye won't hit Pompey again, will ye? Ha, ha, ha! O Lor'! I shall die laffin'. Ha, ha, ha! ho, ho, ho!'

When the steam had cleared away, we all rushed into the saloon. Abel and Mulligan were under the table, writhing in agony. They were very badly scalded about the head and chest. They seemed so stupefied with drink as to be hardly conscious of what had happened. We immediately secured them, and the two seamen also.

Leaving Schniedelhause to guard the captives, we went in a body to the fo'castle. As we passed the galley, Jim the black cook came out and said, 'Welcome back, cap'en; welcome back. I biled de hot water for de darned Yankees, and sarve dem right.'

The sailors were easily secured, as they were all dead drunk. They were sprawling about in all directions. Some had bottles in their hands, or pannikins, from which they had drunk the rum. We clapped them in irons, with the exception of three, who were known to be quiet, inoffensive fellows, from whom no trouble need be expected.

As we were now masters of the vessel, our first care was to get the women and children on board, which we soon did, much to their delight. We then liberated the first and second mates, who had been wounded early in the morning, when the ship was seized. They had been kept on board by Abel in the hope that they would assist him in navigating the ship.

My first care now was to secure my gold, which was scattered about on the table. By dint of great perseverance I was able to pick up nearly the whole of it. I think I only lost a little over an ounce and a half, so I was very well pleased.

Abel, Mulligan, Sam White, and Ben Shakle were put in heavy irons, and watched night and day. They had nothing to eat but bread, and a little meat once a week. After a few days we found that the other men were willing to work. They loudly protested their innocence. We liberated them one by one, and the captain promised that he would never mention the matter against them if they did their duty satisfactorily during the voyage. I must say that after this they behaved well, and were as meek as lambs.

Our success in capturing the ship was mainly due to Pompey, who had suggested the scheme when he whispered to the captain in the boat. He it was, too, who hung out the light to guide us, and he put the rope out at the stern; he stole the pistols and loaded them for our use; he secured the cutlasses and had them in readiness; but the rum was the most potent factor of all.

We all agreed that Pompey should be rewarded, so a subscription was set on foot for him, and the handsome sum of a little over 200*l*. was put down in a few minutes.

We had a very protracted voyage. We were fully a month in rounding the Horn; then we had some favourable weather until we got into latitude 17° North, where we encountered strong easterly gales which drove us up the coast of North America. Our provisions and water were now running short, so the captain determined to put into New York Harbour for a supply. We ran in with a fair wind, and anchored off Staten Island. The Customs officers came on board, but when they learnt for what purpose we had put in, and

that they would not be required, they stopped to
have a yarn with us. With true Yankee inquisi-
tiveness they soon wormed out the story of the
mutiny, and when they heard that the chief ring-
leader was an American, of course they wished to
see him.

The captain took them below and showed them
the prisoners.

'Wall, if this here don't beat cockfighting!
May I never liquor up again if I haven't seen your
ugly phiz before,' said the chief officer to Abel.

'Git out, you fool!' said Abel gruffly.

'I have it! Thunder and lightning! if this
ain't old Slocum, who murdered the bank manager
Chattanooga way, and cut and run with all the
dollars.'

'Bless me!' said the captain; 'what a villain!'

'Yes, sirree; as great a villain as ever respirated.
There's a reward offered for him of five thousand
dollars. Flay me, if I don't make tracks for shore
and claim it. I'll go halves with you, captain.'

'With all my heart,' said the captain. 'I'll be
delighted to get rid of the rascal, you may be sure.
Besides, I don't want any row about this affair when
I get home to London. Why, if it were known that
the ship had been seized I should never get a pas-

senger again, and my owners would assuredly
dispense with my services in future.'

'Done then, captain; it's a bargain. I guess we
had better take the other chap, Mulligan, as you
call him. I'll bet a mint julep he was a pal of
Slocum's, and we may get a round sum for him too.'

'Take him, and welcome,' said the captain.

Abel and Mulligan were taken ashore and lodged
in the Tombs, which is the facetious name for the
Central Prison of New York. Mulligan was, as con-
jectured by the Customs officer, implicated in the
murder of the banker. They were tried, found
guilty, and were hanged soon after. The officer got
the reward for apprehending the murderers, but,
being a cute Yankee and a smart man, did not
make haste to remit the promised moiety to Captain
Googe.

We arrived safely in the Thames after a good
run across. Sam White and Bob Shakle got a month
each for insubordination. The captain would not
charge them with any more serious crime, as he
was afraid he would lose his ship and be ruined if
all the circumstances came out.

We all agreed to keep the matter quiet, so there
was no talk about it at the time. However, as a
good many years have passed since then, I thought

I might safely tell the story just as it happened. I have used fictitious names throughout, so that no one need be offended, or suffer in any way through me.

I may just as well say before I close that I found Mary, Tom, Jack, and Lily as jolly as sand-boys, and right glad we all were to see each other again.

JACK REEVELEY

CHAPTER I

SORROW, misery, and trouble sometimes fasten on a family with a tenacious grip. The sufferers, through their tears, seem to see the heavens falling, and they think God has forgotten them, or, in their despair, imagine that He is nowhere. The clouds are black, the sky is like brass, and all nature is shrouded in gloom. There is no gleam of hope, no ray of comfort. All is gone; nothing left in the world but blank despondency.

Mrs. Reeveley was in such sad case one bright June day. She had been left a widow, in Melbourne, about a fortnight before. Her husband had been long an invalid, and had been confined to bed for months. Their little store of money had been long exhausted, and, bit by bit, their furniture had been sold to pay the rent of the miserable cottage in which they lived, and to provide food and medicine. The loved husband had been laid in the grave, and the grass was beginning to grow over it. Like the prophet Jonah,

she wished she was dead.   She had three children,
Jack, aged eighteen, Annie five, and Lucy three.

She had also living with her a niece and nephew,
Mary, aged sixteen, and Willie twelve, children of a
ne'er-do-weel brother, named Breeve, who had run
away and utterly disappeared.   He had deserted
these children about eleven years before our story
opens, and, from the day he left them, he had not
been heard of.   All inquiries had been baffled.   The
children thought he was dead.   Mr. and Mrs.
Reeveley had taken them and brought them up.
She did not think her brother was dead; she
thought he had deliberately abandoned them, and
she thought he would never come to claim them.

Mrs. Reeveley was a delicate woman with a wan,
pinched face.   Care sat on it, and misery brooded
over it.   She was always anticipating trouble, and
when it came she lay down, metaphorically, and
let it jump on her, and kick her, and cuff her.
When it was gone she would get up, morally limp,
and in evil case.

She sat thus one day after the funeral, rocking
herself to and fro, and she said, 'We have nothing
to eat.   God has forgotten me.'   Annie said,
'Father told me God is everywhere, and He always
hears us.   Tell God, mother, that we are hungry.'

The mother, with tears streaming down her cheeks, fell upon her knees and poured out her heart in prayer. Mary, Willie, and Annie did the same. They were all hungry, and their prayers were earnest. One of them had no doubt that the ceiling would open, and that bread would be showered down before they got up from their knees. What did happen, however, astonished them all, for their landlord, a crusty, crabbed old man, known for his miserly ways, opened the door without knocking, put a basket on the floor, and vanished like a shot. Willie saw him, and said it was Santa Claus. Annie, who expected the blessing, jumped up and said it had come. She lifted the basket with both hands, dragged it to her mother, and shouted, 'I told you, mother, God has not forgotten us. He has sent us plenty to eat.'

There was enough for a week. If anyone says this was not an answer to prayer, but only a chance circumstance, he knows nothing. I have known too many cases of the kind ever to doubt again. God sent the man, just as he sends the stars in their courses. The man said afterwards that he knew the family was starving, and he could not help taking them the basket of food any more than the moon can help going its ceaseless round. Jack happened

to be out at the time, looking for a situation. He
came in soon after, and they all fell to, and ate as
they had not done for many a day. Hunger is a
fine appetiser, and requires no pressing to eat, or
any salt, pepper, or sauce. They had the first, and
wasted no time in looking for the others. When
Jack's sharp hunger was blunted, he said :

'Mother, I've found a situation, and I am to
have a pound a week.'

'I'll never doubt God any more, Jack. He has
been very good to us this day.'

The sun began to shine once more. The moon
was clearer that night, and the stars twinkled more
brightly than Mrs. Reeveley remembered for a long
time. She lay awake for hours, communing with
God, and she thought she was like Thomas, ' of
little faith.' Life is like a kaleidoscope, but the
colours are not usually so bright, or the pattern so
symmetrical. The one is as full of changes as the
other. Life is woven of duller hues and tenderer
tones. Seen ' through a glass darkly,' often
through tears, the view is dreary enough, and the
aspect clouded. To-day does not borrow any relief
from to-morrow. There is neither money in the
purse, nor bread in the basket. Sorrow for the
night does not whisper of joy in the morning.

The blank wall of to-day hides the hope of to-morrow.

Jack was up betimes in the morning. He was the future breadwinner of the family, and he must be up and stirring. He was to be a man of business, and he already thought he heard the twenty shillings chinking in his pocket, and making music like silver bells. No music could be sweeter. On Saturday evenings, when the shutters were up, he would buy a few sweets on his way home, and scatter sunshine among the children as soon as he opened the door.

He took his breakfast quickly, and said good-bye to his mother and the children. He then wended his way citywards as fast as he could, so as to be at the shop in Bourke Street before it was opened. He arrived about five minutes to eight. Before the last stroke of the hour had died away among the clouds, a key was thrust into the lock by his master. Without pausing a moment, the man looked over his shoulder and said:

'Ah! the new boy. Ah! that'll do. Punctual, I see. Punctuality is the soul of business. Yes, and body too. Soul and body. Spirit and flesh. Why, without punctuality this shop would not have been opened at eight o'clock, sun or shower, for twenty long years without missing a day.

II

When you can beat that score, my boy, off your own bat, I'll give you a partnership, with a tenth of the profits. Ha, ha, ha! a joke is like sugar in your tea—it sweetens life, boy; sweetens life.'

John Blenheim the bookseller was a middle-sized man with a slight stoop, caused by leaning forward to read, for he was short-sighted and wore spectacles. He had a pale, thin face, a hook nose, and long, straggling hair. He had a habit of diving into any book that lay nearest his hand, when not serving a customer, and burying his face in it until he heard some fresh footstep coming into the shop; then he would raise his head and look over his spectacles with the last idea, be it grave or gay, still lingering in his eye. The thoughts of the author played on his brain as the wind does on the harp, or as the clay takes the impress of the potter's fingers.

He had never married, and, so far as he knew, had not a relation in the world. He was a lonely man, and was absorbed in making and saving money. People said he hid his money in odd nooks and corners, and that he did not trust banks very much. He always bought for cash. 'Ready money, cash down,' he said. 'Buy in the cheapest market and sell in the dearest; that's my principle, sir.

When you put cash down you can always walk into
the cheapest market, or the market walks to you.
It's a remarkable thing that whenever a man
wants money very badly, it's just at that precise
moment he has goods for sale. That's the exact
time I buy.'

Money-making was his ruling passion ; reading
was his recreation. He was a kindly man withal,
and would even make money sometimes serve a
benevolent purpose. Give me a reading man, and
money-making will not harden his heart altogether.
There is a soft spot somewhere.

The bookseller took Jack round the shop and
showed him where everything was kept. At last
he came to a drawer.

'I always keep this drawer locked,' he said. 'It
has only a few old letters and photos in it ; they are
only for my own eye. It used to be the old sealing-
wax drawer, so I've left " SEALING-WAX " on it still,
to show that it's to be close as wax to everybody
but me.'

'Yes, sir, of course,' said Jack.

Jack determined to be punctual in everything,
and to do his best. He showed great attention to
business. He was quick to learn, and in a few
days could tell where the various articles were

kept. He knew the private marks as if he had known them all his life, and generally proved himself invaluable to the old bookseller, who trusted him more and more as the weeks went past.

One of Jack's duties was to take down the shutters in the morning and put them up at night. One night when he went out to put them up, a man was peering into the shop, his nose flat against the window-pane. He was on tip-toe, and every movement showed intense and absorbing interest, if not downright excitement. The man was terribly in earnest; there could be no doubt about that. Every feature of his face, of which only the left side was visible, was stamped on Jack's brain in a moment. The pattern of the veins that ran over his cheek, like the delta of the Nile on a map, the mole on his chin, which stood out against the light, with three hairs on the top, and the colour of his eyebrows—all were noted by Jack and remembered.

Lost to all besides, the man did not cease staring in at the window till Jack got up one of the shutters; then he turned round, and said, ' That's a fine picture in the window, youngster.'

Then he slunk away, and disappeared among the crowd of aimless and listless people who were sauntering to and fro, without apparently having one single object in life but to kill time. 'I'll know you again,' thought Jack, 'when I see you next time.'

Jack put up the shutters and went inside the shop. The bookseller was fumbling in a curious and furtive manner at the drawer marked 'Sealing-wax.' He shut the drawer as Jack came in, and locked it. Jack thought he heard money chink, and that the bookseller was secreting his cash. Suddenly it flashed across his mind that the man at the window had been watching his master, and that he had done so with no good object.

'I saw a man looking in at the window,' said Jack, 'and he was evidently watching you, sir. He looked like a thief or housebreaker.'

'What was he like, boy? What was he like?'

Jack described him. The bookseller stroked his chin and looked very grave. Jack heard him mutter, 'A bad lot, a bad lot;' then he said aloud, 'I would bet any amount his name begins with a B.'

The boy said nothing. He felt for the old man because he seemed so distressed, and he thought from the remark that the name began 'with a B,' (or that the bookseller guessed so), that the word

in his master's mind must be Blenheim, his own
name, and therefore some relation's. Here was a
discovery. Jack determined to watch and wait
and protect his master's property, because it was
evidently in danger.

'Would you mind, Jack, going next door for
change of a pound ?'

Jack took the pound note and went next door
to the grocer's and got the change, and was soon
back.

The bookseller had evidently been to the same
drawer again, for he was just beside it, and his
hand was going into his pocket with the key, no
doubt. He was whistling a lively air and looking
nervous.

Some things are plain and clear, as the ostrich
is when its head is thrust into a bush. No whistling
or apparent unconcern could hide from Jack the fact
that his master had been to the drawer, and had
put money or valuables into his pocket.

Nothing happened out of the ordinary way for
a few days. The incident of the man at the window
was almost driven out of Jack's head by trouble at
home. His mother was very unwell. She had
caught cold, and it had settled on her lungs. She
coughed frequently, and at night she was worse,

with feverish symptoms and almost incessant cough. She would not send for a doctor because she could not pay him. She did not get up in the morning. So Jack rose very early, lighted the fire, washed and dressed the younger children with the help of Mary, got breakfast ready, made his mother take a cup of tea, and marched off to the shop, punctual as usual.

About one o'clock Mr. Blenheim went to dinner. Almost as soon as he was gone a man marched into the shop. Jack felt something was going to happen. A queer sensation came over him. The presence of the man was somehow baleful. The boy felt it, but could not account for it until he looked round. The man who had flattened his nose against the window pane stood before him.

Jack stared with open mouth, and all the blood in his body seemed to rush to his heart, where it thumped and banged like fifty sledge-hammers. After he had recovered a little from his astonishment he went forward, outwardly cool enough, but inwardly a feverish fire seemed to burn him.

'Would you show me that picture in the window?' said the man.

'Here is one just the same, exactly,' said Jack.

'I have taken a fancy to that one in the window,' said the man, 'and I won't take any other.'

Jack, very unwillingly, put his head between some books, and stretched himself half across the window, and pulled out the picture as quickly as he could. When he got back the man was standing close to the drawer marked 'Sealing-wax.'

'By-the-bye,' said the man, 'I want some sealing-wax.'

Jack went across the shop and brought some.

'Not that sort. I used to get it out of this drawer.'

'We don't keep it there now.'

'Why don't you keep it there now?'

'Because we don't. There's nothing in that drawer.'

'Don't tell me that, my chicken. When there's a Chubb's patent lock on a drawer you mustn't tell me there's nothing in it. People don't keep nothing behind a Chubb. I am accustomed to nothing, and I don't keep it in that safe way. What do you keep in that drawer, my boy?'

'Nothing,' said the boy. 'It's my master's drawer where he keeps his old letters.'

'Walker!' said the man. 'Give me the key, and I'll show you the sealing-wax.'

'I haven't got it,' said Jack.

'No! tight as wax, I see. Well, if I can't get the sealing-wax I used to buy here, I won't take the picture,' and the man stalked out of the shop with his nose in the air.

Jack had felt like a prisoner at the bar all the time the man was in the shop. Now he felt like one reprieved. A load of care seemed to be gone. The clouds had lifted, and the sun shone once more. A flood of song poured through the air from a canary which was warbling in a cage at a neighbour's window. Jack was as happy as the bird. He had passed an ordeal such as he never passed before.

The bookseller came back in about half an hour. Something in the boy's manner struck him as peculiar. He went straight to the drawer. He had some difficulty in getting the key far enough into the lock. He took the key out, poked a pin into it, blew into it, and poked it again. Then he put it in once more and wriggled it about, shook the drawer, and pushed it in by main force. When the key turned in the lock and the drawer opened he looked quite relieved. He examined the receptacle, and appeared to find everything untampered with, but when closing the drawer, observed a bit of wax adhering to the keyhole.

'What's this, boy ?   What's this ?'

Jack told him all about the man ; that he was
the same man who had flattened his face against
the window and had watched him so intently.
Also what the man said about the drawer.
Blenheim shook his head and looked grave.   'This
is a serious matter,' he said.   What could the man
want with the drawer ?   Why should he put wax
on the key-hole ?   To take a cast of it, no doubt ;
to bring a key that would fit the lock ; to come,
some day when only Jack was in the shop, and
either tamper with the boy's honesty or overcome
him by main force, gag him, and rob the place.   Or
could he intend breaking into the shop at night ?
This was worse than all.   This might mean ruin.
He might find money.   He might find many things ;
many old family papers.   This man, too, whom he
knew so well, who was thought to be dead, or many
thousands of miles away !   Now he had suddenly
appeared, and for no good.   It was a bolt out of a
clear sky, an unseen shaft hurtling through the
air, a harbinger of evil.   He could not doubt the
man was drifting into dangerous waters and was
sinking deeper and deeper.   There was a lower
depth coming.   If only he could save him !   He had
once pulled this man out of a quicksand, at the

risk of his own life, when his head only was visible.
If the man had not worn his hair long he could
not have done it. He had saved this man
before, and here he was again, in more need
of saving than ever. He had been smirched
before, with a spot here and there; but now he
seemed black beyond all hope of washing white
again. The base ingratitude of the man, too, who
was going to try his best to rob his benefactor
and friend. This was gratitude! He had read
of a cruel fellow who struck his dog one day by
the side of a deep river. In doing so he fell into
the water and was in danger of drowning, for he
could not swim. The poor animal, following its
instinct or teaching, which it never got from man,
immediately dashed into the river and pulled his
master out; the wretch seized his stick again and
smashed in the faithful creature's skull. This
story came into the bookseller's mind at this
moment. 'Here's a case in point,' he thought.
'Man, thy name is ingratitude!' There have been
men who have died for their friend, and men who
have killed their friend; so far are the poles
asunder. There is no doubt as to the place in the
index which he would have assigned to this man.

Jack noticed that his master was very long in

making his arrangements at shutting-up time.
When the gas was put out, and all ready for
locking up, he said, ' My boy, I've forgotten something,' and he ran back in the dark. He fumbled
about, and moved hastily to and fro. In a few
moments he came back, and quickly locked the
door.

'I've forgotten my pocket-knife,' said Jack.
'Please open the door again and let me get it.'

' Where did you leave it, my boy? '

' On the counter,' said Jack.

' Never mind the knife; you'll get it in the
morning,' and he walked away humming ' All in a
Flowery Vale.'

The bookseller walked up Bourke Street, past
the Eastern Market. The night was dark, but the
street was a blaze of light from the shop windows.
He had just got abreast of one of the lanes of evil
repute in that neighbourhood, when a man
standing at the corner suddenly turned and fled
up the lane. The bookseller saw his face in the
full light that streamed from a window just for a
moment, but that moment revealed the face of a
man he had never forgotten, and never would
forget. The man vanished like a flash; the
darkness swallowed him up. Blenheim ran up

the lane. The glare of the street lights had blinded him for a moment, but he went on in the dark, with his arms out, groping his way, till he came to an open door. He thought he heard someone breathing hard just inside the doorway. In a second he was reeling in the middle of the lane. He had received a blow on the head, and fell heavily to the ground.

CHAPTER II

JACK went home, and not long after supper went to bed. He had to get up in the morning betimes, so he wisely made it a rule to go to bed early. This night his sleep was troubled. He tossed to and fro, muttered to himself, and sometimes cried out in his dreams. He thought he was struggling with the man he had seen in the shop during the day. He thought the man had broken into the shop. He had just time to call 'Police!' and had then closed with the burglar. A long and desperate struggle took place. He awoke in a fright. He was wet with perspiration. His heart beat furiously and his head throbbed painfully.

He got up and looked out. It was intensely dark, excepting now and again when the moon peeped through the heavy clouds which tore along at a great rate in wild confusion. He thought of the shop and the man, and felt an irresistible

impulse to go down to Bourke Street and look at
the place, to see if all was right.   It was clear he
must do something.   The dream was too vivid to
gainsay.

When he got to the shop he thought he saw
someone moving furtively across the road.   He
went over and followed the man, who moved
away as if he did not wish to be seen.   The moon
just looked out, and the boy saw that the man
was his master, and that he seemed feeble and
haggard.

'What are you doing here, boy?'

Jack told him of his dream, and that everything
was so vivid and real he could not rest until he had
come down to see that all was right.

'Come along and see,' said his master.

They silently tried the front door.   It was all
right.   Then they went up the right-of-way at the
side of the building and tried the back door.   It was
locked.   Then they went to the back window.

'By Jove, it's open!' said the bookseller.

In his excitement his spectacles fell off.   He
thrust his head against the casement, and his hat
fell off.   He was just about to get in at the window,
regardless of danger, when he received a terrific
blow on the side of his head, which sent him back

stunned and staggering; a man jumped out and fell over the bookseller. Jack jumped on him, and yelled ' Police !' at the top of his voice, and held on like a bulldog. He grasped the man round the neck and dug his nails into his flesh. He could feel the blood trickling over his fingers. The man felt almost suffocated. The blood rushed to his head. The veins of his neck rose like ropes. His breathing was short and laboured. By a mighty effort he swung himself round, and in doing so almost fell on his hands and knees. Jack rolled round on the man's back, and his legs swayed out like a pendulum. As he felt himself slipping, his right hand caught in the breast pocket of the man's coat, and just prevented him from being thrown off. His left hand clutched the collar of the coat, and by these holds he clung with such a desperate grip that he felt the threads of the cloth buried in his flesh. I have heard of a sailor who fell overboard in a gale who had a rope thrown to him, which he caught and grasped so tightly that when he was hauled up the strands of the rope had so buried themselves in his hands that he could not let go for hours. So it was with Jack. He felt as if he could not let go. Come what might he must hold on. His hand and the cloth seemed welded together, and inseparably fixed. The man writhed and struggled with intense energy. He felt he must get rid of this incubus, this old man of the sea, at all costs. He must sacrifice his coat, at least, if not his liberty. He now thought he heard the police coming, so, making one terrible effort, he dragged Jack by main force to an old fence, and he jumped up, clutched the top, and had the satisfaction of feeling the boy fall off his back. He tumbled over the other side; as he did so he turned his face. The moon shone out. He was a negro, as black as soot.

Jack fell, but he carried off the right sleeve and breast pocket of the man's coat. It tore clean away. If it had not the boy must have gone over the fence on the man's back. When Jack recovered himself, he made a dash at the fence, and scrambled over in pursuit of the robber, but he had vanished. The darkness had swallowed him up and he was gone. Jack felt it was useless to proceed further in chase of the man. He went over the fence again, and began to think of his master who lay groaning where he had fallen. He helped him up. He said he was bruised, but he thought no bones were broken. He felt faint and weak. Jack said he would soon recover, and tried to cheer him up by

I

saying he thought the robber had carried off no
plunder.

'Get me some water, Jack.'

Jack jumped through the open window, and
brought a tumbler of water. The bookseller drank
some, and bathed his forehead with the rest. Then
he walked about a little, and soon felt stronger.
Jack said he would go inside the shop and fasten
the window, then get out by the front door. The
bookseller went round and opened it for him.

The boy had to do all the thinking. He now
proposed that they should light the gas, and go
round the shop to see whether anything had been
taken away.

They lit the gas. Boylike, Jack looked for the
knife he had left on the counter the night before.
It was nowhere to be seen. The man must have
taken it.

'I'll know it again,' said Jack. 'My initials
are on it.'

The bookseller hurriedly put his hand on several
hiding-places where he had secreted money. None
of them had been interfered with. He then went
to the sealing-wax drawer. It had been forced and
its contents lay scattered about.

'Ha, ha, ha!' laughed the bookseller. 'I was

too cunning for him. He hasn't got a penny. The man with the mole on his chin is done this time.'

'It wasn't him,' said Jack. 'It was a negro, as black as my hat.'

'There are plenty of white men under a black skin when they want to disguise themselves. Your friend with the mole is up to any dodge.'

'He was a black fellow, no mistake about that,' said Jack. 'Anyway, I've got a piece of his coat which tore off in the struggle I had with him. It might lead to his discovery.'

'Let me see it,' said the bookseller. 'Read out the description, and I will take it down in writing.'

'Piece of an old coat,' said Jack; 'right sleeve and pocket, nothing in it.'

'Just like him,' muttered the bookseller to himself.

'Cloth frayed and threadbare.'

'Like his character, fits him to a tee.'

'Check pattern.'

'Exact again: checked this time.'

'And stripes,' said Jack.

'Deserves them richly.'

'Now, that's all,' said Jack. 'I'll put it away till to-morrow.'

He put it away under the counter. While doing

I 2

so, he saw a letter lying on the floor. It was yellow
with age. He lifted it up and spread it on the
counter. He looked at it long and carefully. He
knew the writing. Yes, he knew it. It was his
mother's writing, there could be no doubt about
that. He turned white as a sheet, and fell down in
a dead faint.

When he revived a little, he saw the bookseller
bending over him, and dashing water in his face.

'My poor boy, this night's work is too much
for you.'

'It isn't that,' said Jack. 'I saw one of my
mother's letters on the floor; I am sure it was
hers. I would know her writing anywhere, and it
was signed with her maiden name. Where could
it have come from?'

'All fancy, my boy, all fancy. What tricks our
imaginations play us! First you say the robber
was a black man, now you say you saw a letter
written by your mother. You see there is no letter
here,' and he pointed to the counter. 'Perhaps
you will believe it is all imagination.'

'It must be a trick of my fancy,' thought the
boy. 'I must have imagined it when I fainted.'

He soon recovered, and the first thing he did
was to look round furtively for the letter. It was

gone. The bookseller had slipped it into his pocket. They now put out the gas and locked the door.

The events here recorded did not occupy half an hour; no policeman had appeared on the scene, although the gas-light must have shone through the chinks of the door. They walked up Bourke Street very slowly and silently. Not a word passed between them. Each had thoughts running through his brain which gave much food for reflection. The morning might bring some light on what now seemed dark and confused. A policeman at last hove in sight.

'Tell the policeman of the robbery,' said Jack.

'No, no, my boy, keep it quiet. I don't want it to be known. Tell no one; I begin to suspect that it will be better for both you and me to say nothing about it.'

Jack made no reply. He could not understand the case in the least. It was a tangled skein, of which he had got the wrong end; a maze to which he had not got the right turning. He was fogged, and wholly in the dark.

They walked slowly. Jack seemed to lead, and he mechanically went homewards. He expected the bookseller to branch off at every turning, but he kept plodding on by his side. They were getting

near the boy's home, and he did not want to show his
master the meanness of it.   They came abreast of
the house, and Jack had almost made up his mind
to walk past it, when his master suddenly said :

'Where do you live, my boy ?'

Jack would not tell a lie, so he said, 'Here, this
is our house.'

'Well, I've seen you home safely.   So good
morning.   Be down at eight o'clock as usual.'

At that moment a man ran away from Jack's
window, and dashed past them.   Jack made a
clutch at him, but got a bad hold, as he was taken
unawares.   It was sufficient, however, to check the
man's career.   He looked round and gave the boy
a blow on the chest which sent him staggering into
the gutter.   He turned his head to see what had
become of the boy.   Jack saw his face clearly ; the
sleeve of his coat was gone.   He was the man who
broke into the shop, that was plain ; but he was a
white man.

The bookseller ran to help the boy up.   He set
him on his feet, and said, 'More thieves, my boy !
The world is full of them.   They meet you at every
turn.   Are you hurt, my boy ?'

'No, I didn't feel the blow a bit.   Good morning,
sir.   I'll be down at eight.'

Jack let himself in by the window, which he had left unfastened. He found the room all in confusion. The man had ransacked the whole place. Could he have come after his missing coat-sleeve, thought Jack, and could he really be the same man he had encountered at the shop. It was possible, of course, as his master had hinted, that the robber had blackened his face as a disguise, and had since washed it. The robber evidently knew that Jack lived here, and had come to the house, as soon as he could, to recover the coat-sleeve, which would perhaps be the means of identifying him, and bringing him to punishment. He had heard of a policeman being so sharp as to be able to say, when he saw a shred of cloth hanging to a hook in a jeweller's shop, 'I once saw Bill Sikes, or Tommy the Screw, wearing a coat of this pattern,' and then go away with a pair of handcuffs in his pocket, and come back with the man, fit the shred of cloth to the coat, and charge him with robbery, recover the jewellery, and get the man convicted, and all by the scrap of cloth.

The man had come looking for the coat-sleeve. The boy thought it was a good thing he had not been in bed and asleep. Perhaps the man was desperate, and would have murdered him. He

fastened the window, and drove a nail into the
sash to prevent it being opened. He then jumped
into bed, but he could not sleep. He got up early,
prepared breakfast, and helped to wash and dress
the children. Then he made his way to the shop.
His master had not arrived. He looked at the post
office clock and found it was five minutes to eight.
He leant against the shop door, and was almost
asleep, when his master put his hand on his
shoulder, and said :

'Nothing the worse for your rough-and-tumble
last night, I hope ? '

' No,' said the boy, ' but I feel very sleepy.'

The bookseller opened the door. The shutters
were taken down, the floor was swept, and the
business of the day was fairly begun, before Jack
began to think of the exciting scenes of the night
before. The only clue to the robber was the coat-
sleeve. He took it from under the counter, and
spread it out on a table. There was a pocket, but
nothing in it, no information there. He passed
his hand all down the seams. The lining was
thick, and there was a good deal of padding. He
ripped the seams with a pair of scissors, and
inserted his hand between the lining and the cloth.
He felt something which was neither cloth nor

paper. It was too big to pull out through the opening he had made, so he cut away some more stitches. Then he pulled out a large piece of parchment and unfolded it. It was evidently an official document of some sort; there were seals and stamps on it, and it related to a piece or parcel of land: so much Jack could make out at a glance. The folds of the parchment were frayed and worn, as if by much rubbing, and there were discolourations here and there. Jack was about to begin a careful reading of the document, when he felt warm breathing on his cheek. He looked up, and felt, rather than saw, that the bookseller was leaning over him, and that he was much excited.

'My God, what is this?' said the bookseller.

His face became ashy pale; he clutched the counter wildly, and would have fallen, had not Jack caught him in his arms and held him up.

The bookseller very soon recovered; he pulled the parchment towards him and pored over it in a dazed sort of way. He breathed hard, and tried to speak once or twice.

Jack was alarmed. He gently slid his master into a chair, and ran for a glass of water which he put to the man's lips, and then moistened his brow.

In a few minutes his master revived and gradually became more self-possessed.

'You do not know what you have done for me, my boy. You have brought peace and happiness to me, life and joy. I seem to have everything now I could wish for. This parchment is the title to the land on which this shop is built. It was stolen from me years ago. The whole property is mine. It belonged to a partner, but I bought him out. He executed the deed in due form, and one night he robbed me, and stole the title ; now it has been restored to me by your means, my boy, in a most wonderful manner.'

'I'm very glad,' said the boy.

'So you may, Jack, so you may. I am pleased to hear you say so. I'm the gladdest man in Melbourne to-day. I want you to be the gladdest boy in the city, so I want you to run home and tell your mother that you are my partner from to-day. We'll paint up over the door, Blenheim and Reeveley. I'll tell everybody that you made more money in a few minutes than I have made in twenty years. Now we'll lock up the shop. Come with me, and I'll lodge the title with a banker I know. I defy the negro then to get it.'

The old man put the parchment in his pocket,

then locked the door. They walked down to Collins Street, and turned into a bank. The bookseller went into the manager's room, and asked him to lock up the title deed in his strong room. He soon came back to the boy, and clapped him on the back, and said, 'We are the funniest partners in the city, and the happiest. The business is worth 50,000*l.*, does not owe a shilling, and I make over a quarter of it to you. Run home now, and tell your mother. And look here,' he said, calling the boy back, and slipping a handful of sovereigns into his pocket; 'I'll look out for the best house I can find for your mother, and we'll get her into comfortable quarters soon. I'll send a doctor to see her, and tell him what to do.'

The bookseller hurried away, and the boy went homewards as one who dreamed. He pulled out one of the sovereigns, and looked at it. He dropped it in, and brought out another, and another, and weighed them, and tried to bend them, and smelt them. They were made of gold, no doubt. So much was in evidence of the bookseller's good will; but there are day dreams as well as night dreams, which tinge the hill-tops of life with brightest hues, and the day brings forth nothing but the veriest neutral tints or sober black.

However, the boy was glad, and his master was glad. This was plain, and the gladness of both was the direct outcome of the fight with the robber. This was clear. The title deed was evidence. The whole thing was coherent and plain, and the bookseller was going to reward him.

He held up his head and walked on. He began to whistle. His face was radiant: a passing boy called out to him, 'What's up? Is your grandmother dead and left you a fortune?' This brought him down from the clouds. He was walking once more upon the earth, but he felt, somehow, that his prospects were solid as the ground.

He went into a shop and bought a black bag.

A man with sovereigns in his pocket must be respectable. At first he thought of a basket, but that was not good enough. He wanted to buy a lot of things and take them home—some luxuries for his mother, and some presents for Mary and the children. He went into a grocer's shop and purchased a lot of delicacies for his mother, and some nice things for the children. A jeweller's shop attracted him next. A brooch for Mary would be rather nice. He thought girls liked such things. It would be pleasant to pin one on at her throat, and give her a kiss at the same time. Mary was

the most beautiful girl in the world and the best.
He had never seen anyone more beautiful, and he
had never seen any better. He bought a brooch;
just the one Mary would like, he thought. He
strode along homewards. He was happy, and was
going to dispense happiness. 'It is more blessed
to give than to receive.' Thinking of it made his
face shine. Presently he saw some toys hanging
in a window. Good idea! he would get some.
In another minute he had a box of tea things, a
Noah's ark, a ball, and a bleating lamb in one
hand, and the black bag in the other. He was
soon at home, and was surrounded. His mother
was better. Package after package was taken out of
the bag. Parcel after parcel was opened, and the
various toys were distributed. Every one was
happy. 'Mary, come here,' said Jack; and he ran
into another room. Mary followed him. The girl
was blushing like a rose. The brooch was pinned
on, and the kiss given. Boy and girl were radiant.
It was a lovely world, full of rainbows and sunshine. Jack had much to tell his mother. He
was a second Aladdin, and had found the wonderful
lamp. Like Midas, everything he touched had
turned into gold.

CHAPTER III

Jack noticed, next day, that the bookseller was as
restless as a bee in springtime, and as busy. A
kindly light shone in his eyes : a beaming smile
lurked about his mouth, and played all over his
face like summer lightning. His step was more
springy than usual. He had shed the sere and
yellow leaf, and he suddenly began to look ten
years younger.

He was in and out of the shop all day. He had
no sooner come in than he wanted to go out again,
and his absences were longer and longer. This
went on for a few days. Jack's curiosity was
aroused, but he said nothing. Time would show
what all this meant.

On the fifth day the bookseller came to the
shop, and sat down with a sigh of satisfaction.

'Jack,' said he, 'I have found a house for you.'

'For me !' said Jack.

'Well, for your mother then. I want her to

get away from that unhealthy hole she is in. We'll get her plump and strong again, Jack. We'll get the light in her eye, and the roses on her cheeks, in no time, in no time, boy.'

The bookseller told Jack that he had bought a cottage for his mother. It was quite a picture, embowered in trees and flowers. It was all furnished, 'spick and span' new. He put the key in Jack's hand, and told him what house it was. When Jack comprehended, he was almost speechless, for he remembered that once, in passing it, he had told his master that he thought it was the most beautiful house he had ever seen.

'A furniture van will be at your house to-morrow morning,' said the bookseller. ' Your mother might like to take all her things to the new house. Get everything removed by twelve o'clock to-morrow, and I'll send a carriage punctually at twelve to take her and the children to the house.'

'Oh! you are too good,' said Jack. The glistening tears stood in his eyes. 'I cannot thank you just now, but I will show my thankfulness by loving you, and serving you, all my days.'

'That's right, my boy, that's right. We'll have many happy ones.'

The boy thought of his mother, and of all the

possibilities of renewed health and happiness.
Hitherto her life had been dark and dreary.
Very little light had shone into it; no joy and
no peace. All had been hard. Her path had been
rocky. Now, God had smiled upon him, and blessed,
and led, and guided him, and he thanked Him for
all His blessings and all His goodness.

Next day the furniture van appeared. Jack had
told his mother of the new house he was going to
take her to, but he let her know that his master
had bought it for her, and furnished it. He lauded
him to the skies, as the kindest man in the world.

Mrs. Reeveley shook her head. She did not
understand it all. The clouds were breaking too
rapidly, and the sunshine was coming too quickly.
She had made up her mind that this world was a
vale of tears, and, if it had not turned out as watery
as she expected, she determined on keeping it as
damp as she could.

The furniture was packed in the van, and the
last rope was tied by the vanman. He mounted
his perch, cracked his whip, and the vehicle lum-
bered down the street, and swayed to and fro. The
mattresses nodded to the magpie, and the magpie
was pulled up short by an extra jolt, just as he had
started the first bar of 'There's nae Luck about the

House.' He gave it up as a bad job, and sulked in the bottom of his cage.

The carriage arrived in due course. It was a large and handsome one, and was drawn by two fine upstanding horses, well groomed and beautifully harnessed. Mrs. Reeveley, Mary, and the children got in. The coachman drove away. The horses seemed to fly. The houses and trees appeared to waltz past. The very clouds looked as if they rolled away. It was an enchanting and bewildering ride to all of them. The children's eyes danced with joy. Mary smiled. Even Mrs. Reeveley condescended to relax one muscle, which undid the severe and sorrowful expression which usually hovered over her mouth in a chronic down-curve.

They reached their new house at last. It had a new look about it. It was newly painted and newly furnished. The lawn was newly cut and the hedge was newly trimmed.

The bookseller waited for a few days until Mrs. Reeveley had got a little accustomed to the house. One morning he asked Jack how his mother liked it, and whether she was getting stronger.

'Oh yes,' said Jack, 'she likes the house immensely, and her health is improving every day. Her cough is almost gone. She has a better appe-

K

tite. She sleeps well, and she is happier than I have seen her for a long time.'

'That's right, that's right,' said the bookseller; 'do you think I may go and see her to-day?'

'Yes,' said Jack, 'she said she would like to see you; in fact, she said she would call at the shop to thank you for all you have done for us. She is always saying she cannot understand it all. She has some idea that she must have known you ever so long ago, when she was quite young, before she was married. She says she knew a Mr. Blenheim longer ago than she can remember, and wonders whether you can be any relation, or whether you are really the same gentleman she knew.'

'Yes, I'm the same; I'm the same,' said the bookseller, in an absent and abstracted way; 'the same old John Blenheim, with the same old thoughts of her. I can see her now, as she was twenty years ago. I wonder whether she is like that; whether she would know me, a grizzled and grey old fellow. I always think of her as still young and beautiful. Oh! the days that are gone; oh! the days that are gone.'

Jack caught words here and there, and tried to piece them together, but found it as difficult as joining a letter which had been torn into a thousand fragments. Lives are just like rings in the water, caused by a stone thrown in. They fly apart and take their own course, but some day, and perhaps far off, they mix and mingle, and become united— like a mountain stream which runs for many miles as one, but becomes separated into many channels, and, at last, meets and mingles in the great ocean. So is life. Like clouds blown hither and thither returning whence they came to bless the earth. Ships that had sailed on the same day may meet long after in mid-ocean. Fragments of a broken world may, after whirling for ages, lie side by side as dust upon this earth, and talk of the far-off time.

The bookseller dressed himself in his best, and, for a wonder, walked with his head erect; a smile on his face, and a merry tune in his heart. His eyes twinkled, and his spectacles reflected the twinkle and broke up every separate twinkle into a thousand sparkles. If we could have seen through his spectacles we would have beheld a fair world. Every boy and girl an angel, the sky bluer, the sun brighter and the air balmier than Garden of Eden times. He went on and on, but steering straight for the one house he was thinking of, and the one woman he had thought of ever since he was a boy.

He soon came to the gate. It took a long time

to open. The catch was unaccountably stiff, or his hand was unusually tremulous. At last he got it open and went in. His heart beat, and his footsteps seemed to crunch the gravel into powder, and sound like thunder. Slowly but surely he reached the door; then he felt cooler and calmer, and more his usual self. He rang the bell, and all the ironmongery in the world seemed to have broken loose, and be coming down stairs in a hurry to meet him.

After an age, as it seemed, someone came to the door. It was Mary. He stammered out:

'Is Mrs. Reeveley at home?'

'Yes,' said Mary; 'walk in, sir.'

He walked in as he was told. He would have done anything just then he had been told. He would have gone away if he had been told.

Mrs. Reeveley came into the room with a flush on her cheeks, and something of her old girlish manner.

'Mary, don't you know me?'

'No! Can it be? Are you John Blenheim I used to know long ago?'

'I am the same John Blenheim; yet changed, yet changed; not quite the same, not quite the same.'

'Let me thank you from the bottom of my

heart for all your wonderful kindness to my boy, and for all you have done for me and mine,' she said faintly. She had sunk down into a chair, and was holding her hand over her heart. Every particle of colour had left her face. She seemed to be fainting. The bookseller sprang to her side, and caught her in his arms as she was falling. He did not know what to do any more than a three months old baby, but she did not fall out of his arms. He held her firmly enough. The colour came slowly back to her face. Her eyes opened, and she smiled; actually smiled, when she saw the look of wonder and amazement with which he regarded her.

'I am better now,' she said. 'It was only the sudden thoughts that came back after so many years. Just the remembrances, like bells pealing from far over the water.'

She sat with her eyes half-closed, pondering, thinking, dreaming, as she thought of the days that had gone, of the years that had flown away. No single incident of her life dominated another. All seemed to fly, hither and thither, through her brain, to and fro, like a weaver's shuttle, or like summer lightning playing at hide-and-seek among the clouds. Sometimes she saw her husband, in his early manhood, whom she had loved so much, and mourned so deeply, wooing her as of old, and looking so handsome and good. Then she thought of John Blenheim, and how he had loved her, and was true and noble, and how sorry she was for him, for she had liked him, and admired him, and knew he was one of the best of men. Then she thought of the time when she stood at the altar as a bride; the perfume of the orange-blossom swept past her fresh and sweet, as it did, oh! so many years ago, and she thought she heard the pealing of the organ as she went out of church proudly leaning on her husband's arm.

Suddenly she came down from dreamland, and found herself in this world of joy and sorrow, life and death. The bookseller was looking at her curiously, and wondering what he would do next. He coughed and cleared his throat, for there was something in it that comes when people are touched with sympathy or emotion, or when tears are ready to overflow their banks. Why such a prosaic food-gulping and drink-swallowing place feels in this fine and noble way, who can tell? No one. There it is, and there it was in the bookseller's throat. He cleared it away at last, and said:

'Mary, cheer up. The clouds are breaking, the sun is shining, and I hope sorrow and sighing have passed away. I think you are going to be happy now. Jack is a treasure; everything has prospered with me since he came to me. I look upon him as the foundation of all the prosperity that has come upon me. I trust him with everything, and that is the reason I have made him my partner. He will have a fair income. He is a good son, and he will make you happy. If you will let me try to make you happy too, I shall be the most fortunate of men.'

They sat together late into the afternoon. The servant who came in to light the gas said, afterwards, that she was sure something was up with Missus. 'She is so happy like.'

The bookseller went away humming 'All in a Flowery Vale.' Peace in his heart, joy on his face. The sun was setting in flaming vermilion, and scattering splashes of the same on gable ends, chimney pots, tree tops, tips of telegraph poles, high window panes, and church steeples. When these hot tints had faded, they appeared higher up among the clouds, gilding them, burnishing them, and illuminating them, like some missal of olden times that an artist monk had pored over, and painted, and stippled, and left as his masterpiece.

The bookseller looked up, and said aloud 'The heavens declare the glory of God and the firmament showeth His handiwork.' 'I beg your pardon,' said a slouching street lamp supporter who had nothing else to do, and did it. 'Oh!' said the bookseller, 'I was only admiring the sky.'

'Thought you looked a fool,' said the man; 'the colour of a nip o' brandy is more richer. If you come round the corner and have some we'll talk about colour.'

The bookseller said nothing. He walked away, looking down sadly as he went. All the bright tints had gone out of the sky since this lump of common clay had spoken to him.

'Miserable brute! I pity you from the bottom of my heart. Your life is out of harmony. You have no poetry in your soul. Neither form, nor colour, nor drawing in your besotted, inane uppermost end—I wouldn't call it head for the world. Wretched brandy cask, go thy way. Faugh!'

He felt better after delivering himself thus. His step resumed its buoyancy. His stick began to twirl. He hummed his favourite tune, and he walked on briskly. He turned into Bourke Street, and went westwards. The shop windows were lighted. The street lamps were being lit. Many busy feet were hurrying on, some with silent tread from leanness of leather, others with vulgar creak

from too much fatness of it. Shopgirls and seam-
stresses were going eastward to tea. Workmen
and their wives were wending theatrewards as fast
as they could to secure a good place in the pit.
Publicans in their shirt-sleeves were standing at
their doors, like fat spiders waiting for their prey.
Newspaper boys, with nimble feet and glib tongue,
were proclaiming the news. Matchsellers were
uttering their monotonous chant, and blind beggars
were tapping the pavement with their stick, as
they felt their way.

When the bookseller was seized by an idea it
stuck to him, and he stuck to it. He looked at it
from every point, as an artist looks at a view before
he begins to sketch it. He strove with it, and
wrestled with it, as a gladiator might with his foe :
or he coaxed it, or played with it, just as the idea
warranted, or the mood took him. To-day an idea
had him in its grip, and he was willing that it
should be so. While the sunlight lasted he was
content, but now that the last tinge of colour had
left the sky, and the prosaic yellow gas lights
asserted themselves, thoughts of the shop, and Jack,
began to flit through his brain. The solid paving-
stones of the footpath were under his feet; the
roar and rattle of the street were in his ears;

the smells of gutters were in his nostrils; and the dust of the street was in his eyes and mouth.

Suddenly the shop window seemed to jump into sight. Jack stood at the door. He had been looking impatiently up and down the street in the hope that his partner would soon appear. Jack always thought of him as his master still, for the word partner, and all it meant, seldom crossed his brain.

Jack was glad to see him, and said so, for shutting-up-time had come and gone, and the boy had been anxiously waiting for him. Now he had come he called the shopboy, for they had got one since the partnership began, and told him to put up the shutters. Jack helped him, for he was not above doing as he had done so long. When everything was ready the gas was put out. The shopboy went his way, whistling shrill and clear, happy that the day's work was over and done with. The bookseller closed the door with a bang, and locked it. Jack turned the handle, and tried whether the bolt had shot in the lock. They then said good night. Jack turned to the right and the bookseller to the left, and they took their several ways.

When Jack reached home he found his mother

and Mary sitting on the verandah, enjoying the lovely evening. The garden looked like paradise to Mary. The gravel walk was the 'Golden Street,' and the Norfolk Island pine in the centre bed was the 'Tree of Life,' and there was to be no sorrow and sighing any more.

Mrs. Reeveley kissed her son as usual, and he sat down beside her. Mary nestled up on the other side. The mother was in high spirits, and chatted and laughed for a long time. Her invalid days seemed over. Ever since she came to the new house she had improved in health. Her appetite was good, and her cough was gone. Prosperity, with whip and spur, had left her troubles behind. She had escaped from Giant Despair, and she was walking in the land of Beulah.

The bookseller was a frequent visitor, and he often came to spend the evening. After a while he was looked on as one of the family. If by any chance he missed coming for a day, his absence was talked about. His ring at the door was looked for. The children hung on his coat tails, and climbed on his knees. He often had picture-books in his pocket for them, or sweets, or fruit. He seldom came empty-handed, and he was looked upon as a fairy godfather, who had only to wish and put his hand behind his back, and pull out present after present for them.

A few months went past very swiftly. The bookseller had established himself as prime favourite with every member of the household. He had visibly changed in his appearance. His clothes no longer hung upon him as they hung on the clothes-pegs. They fitted him. They were of newer cut and more fashionable material. His hair and beard were trimmed *à la mode*. His boots were from Paris ; and his hat, the crucial test of all, was one of Christie's best. His stoop was almost gone, and his step was springy. His tally of years seemed all wrong, and he suddenly appeared to go back ten years, like the shadow of Hezekiah's sundial. As he looked so spruce and youthful his friends would stop him in the street and say, 'Hullo! Blenheim, what's up? Going to be a boy again ; ' or, 'Taken a new lease ; ' or, 'Going to be married, old boy ! '

He bore all this chaff with his blandest smile and the utmost good-nature, and laughed and chuckled to himself, and went his way humming 'All in a Flowery Vale.'

Mrs. Reeveley noted all these signs, and she thought something was going to happen. Every day seemed to bring it nearer. Winter was past. The trees and plants were putting forth buds, and a flood of sunshine and song was about to burst forth.

One day she and the bookseller were walking in the garden, aimlessly apparently, but not so. He was gradually leading her towards a summer-house embowered in creepers. When they reached it, he took her hand, and led her in, and they sat down.

Love is too holy for intrusion. A coach and horses would not drag out of me a single word of what was said. I would rather be broken on the wheel than divulge a syllable. I would rather be banished to Siberia than write a sentence of the conversation. It will ever be a close secret with me, and it will go down to the grave with me. I will only say that, when they came out, there was an extra tinge of colour on their cheeks, and an extra light in their eyes, and that light was the light of love, which has ever been in the world, since the morning stars sang together, and ever will be till time shall be no more.

The wedding was a quiet one. Jack was the 'best man,' and Mary was the bridesmaid. There was not a happier household in Melbourne that day.

CHAPTER IV

Some months afterwards, Jack's mother lost the
key of one of her drawers, and she asked him to
bring a bunch from the locksmith's, so that she
might get a new key. When he came back at
night, she was busy, and she asked him to take the
keys he had brought, and see if one of them would
fit the lock. He went into the next room, and he
soon had the drawer open. He pulled it out, boy
like, to its full length. The first thing that caught
his eye was a photograph. Curiosity made him
look at it. It was a face he had seen before. It
had been photographed on his brain, one night, and
he had never forgotten it. There was a mole on
the chin, with three hairs in the centre. The face
was that of the man who had flattened his nose
on the shop window pane, and who had taken an
impression of the keyhole of the drawer marked
' sealing-wax.'

All the blood in Jack's body began to rush into his face, and the next minute it began to course back again. He turned white as death and cold as marble, and fell down with a crash.

His mother jumped up in a fright, and ran into the room. She called 'Mary!' and nearly went off in a swoon herself. Mary came flying into the room, and seeing Jack on the floor, ghastly white, she ran to him and lifted his head, and rested it on her lap, and called for water. When it was brought, she dashed some in his face, and moved him gently to and fro. In a few minutes he opened his eyes and looked wildly round. Then he closed them again and lay thinking. At first he thought he had seen the man in the room. Then he remembered the photograph.

Jack was just going to ask his mother about the photograph when Mary's scared face caught his eye. Something checked his curiosity, and he set his teeth tight, and closed his lips. He must take another opportunity, but he determined he would not sleep that night until he had found out how the photograph had got into his mother's drawer, and who the villain was, for he knew him to be villain, and that of the deepest dye.

Mary soon left the room. She had barely shut

the door when Jack said, ‘Mother, who is that
man ? ’

‘ What man ? ’

‘ The man whose photo I saw in your
drawer.’

‘ That is your uncle, my boy.’

‘ Mary’s father ? ’

‘ Yes.’

‘ That’s impossible !　I could not believe it.
Never ! ’

‘ I know it’s a bad likeness, and very far from
flattering.　Certainly, Mary does not take after
him, but she is the image of what her mother was
at her age.’

‘ Where is he now?　When did you see him
last ? ’

‘ I have not seen him for many years.　I think
he must be dead.’

‘ Do you mean to say he is your brother ? ’

‘ Yes.’

‘ My poor dear mother.’

Mother and son looked into each other’s eyes
for a moment, and they began to cry and sob
bitterly.　The humiliating truth had burst upon
him in all it hideousness.　He was the nephew of
a midnight robber, who, but for God’s mercy,

might have been a murderer, too. He told his mother the whole story.

'Yes,' said his mother, 'he was a partner of Mr. Blenheim years ago, and I have heard he cheated him and wronged him ; but he was forgiven, time after time, until the breach was too wide for forgiveness to bridge, and he went out into the night, and passed, as I thought, from our ken for ever. Oh ! what shall I do ! What shall I do !'

'I believe Mr. Blenheim would forgive him even now,' said Jack ; 'I believe he would do anything for him. Oh, mother, if I could bring him back to honest ways, and restore him again, for Mary's sake, how happy I should be !'

'I had a message from him once, from Ballarat, I think, when he was in terrible straits for money. I sent him my last farthing, and I have never heard of him since.'

'I hope he is dead,' said Jack, 'but that is too good to be true. I don't think this is quite right, mother, and I ought not to say it, but I could not help it, the words just came out because the thoughts were there. The bell rings, for something makes it, and the thoughts come clanking on my tongue because they are in my heart.'

'He was once as pure and good as you, my son,

L

but he fell, bit by bit; temptation was too strong for him; bad companions led him astray. If he could only be reasoned with, if only we could find him and help him, and put him on the right track. I think it would not be difficult to keep him on it if we once had him among us again. We would lavish all our kindness on him, and the children would love him, and kiss him back into forgiveness and happiness once more.'

'Mother, for your sake and Mary's, I would like to help him. It goes against the grain; but it must be done, and at once, or it may be too late. I ought to go and look for him, and tell him you love him still. I will speak to Mr. Blenheim; perhaps he will not discourage the idea. Perhaps he will let me go for a month to make inquiries. Perhaps I may be successful.'

It has been ever so since the world began. The good have had to weep for the bad, and carry their burden, and hush up their sorrow. There was an Abel and a Cain, a Solomon and an Absalom, who spread a blessing or a curse on the family name. No one knows what was suffered before the crash came, what tears and cries, what schemes for reform, what bands of love stronger than death, striving with the vile and the erring. Tears and blood and broken hearts, lamentation and woe, sorrow and sighing, down the weary ages.

Jack's uncle, the man Breeve, with the mole on his chin, had skated over thin ice since his early manhood. He had camped with sin and made his bed with iniquity. Drink was his besetting vice. When he had money he soaked it up like a sponge. Sometimes he made good resolutions, but the sponge wiped them out quick and clean. He had absorbed all the vices of all the Breeve family for generations, just to show how many unclean spirits he could dwell with in his devilment. Many a kind mother and loving sister or wife have tried to save such a man. It has been done, thousands of times, by the help of God. Without it, it is mopping out the Atlantic. Let no man or woman try it in their own strength.

Jack spoke to Mr. Blenheim next day on the subject. His voice faltered and his cheek burned. He knew now that his master was well aware, all the time, who this man was, and why he had not denounced him and handed him over to the police. It had been for his mother's sake, and because the man had been his partner.

Blenheim sighed and shook his head. 'No use, I'm afraid; no use. Let sleeping dogs lie. Don't

wake the lion. He's better away—better away. I'm
afraid he'll only be a grief to your mother, my boy.
I would forgive him fast enough, but I could not
forgive him if he embitters her life. She's happy now.
Let the sun shine. · Keep out the hurricane's roar
and the lightning's flash. I'm a man of peace.'

The bookseller opened a drawer and turned
over some papers. He selected one, and handed
it to Jack. The boy took it and read it carefully.
It was a report by a private detective, who was
sent on the track of Breeve soon after the shop
was broken into. The bookseller had actually
commissioned the detective, whom he knew and
trusted, to seek out the man and offer him help—
to relieve his necessities, to set him up in some
business, or to send him small sums of money
from time to time. This is the detective's report.

'Traced B—— to Flemington, where he lay
concealed in a wood-house. He was seen leaving
it about daylight. He made his way across country,
carefully avoiding roads and houses. He was seen
at one or two points by people I interviewed.
Picked up a shred of cloth, torn from his trousers,
on a stringy bark fence he crossed. Cloth here-
with, which I recognise as part of the trousers he
had on when last seen in Bourke Street. He

seems to have called at a low shanty at Keilor, and taken dinner, same day. I was satisfied, from the description, that he was the man. " Mole on chin and three hairs on it." Enough for me. The man went west, across Keilor plains, in the direction of Ballarat. I walked over the plains, same direction, looking for " sign." Saw many " one-man " encampments, with remains of charred wood, where a fire had been lit. Poked about the places. Nothing clear or definite. Hurried on, over the dreary waste, without meeting any one to inquire of. Reached Bacchus Marsh, and slept there all night. Inquiries of no use here. Police could have told me all I wanted, but you warned me not to communicate with them. I walked up main road, and came to a baker's shop, with three loaves in the window, and a bag of flour at the door. " Likely place," said I. " Just the place for a hungry man to call." So I went in and bought a loaf from the baker's wife. Pretended I was hungry and began to eat it. I said, " This is splendid bread." " Yes," said the woman, " the best bread out of Melbourne, or in it for that matter." " So a man told me," says I, " who bought a loaf here a short time ago. Perhaps you remember the man." " What was he like ? "

says she. "If you ever saw him," says I, "you
would remember him. He has a mole on his
chin with three hairs on it." Lucky shot of
mine. The woman gave a start. "Oh! that
man! He looked like a man down on his luck,
or hiding from the police." "Oh no," says I,
"he's a millionaire, and goes about the country
in disguise." "Oh dear, man," says she, "if I had
known that I would not have been so short with
him. I was glad enough to see the last of the
mole, and the broad of his back, as he went up
the hill." "Good morning," says I. "I suppose
he was going to Ballarat." "I suppose so," she
said, "for my husband saw him in Ballan next
day." I had picked up the clew, and I knew the
end of the thread was at Ballan. I walked on
slowly, hoping some man would be making my
way with a vehicle and give me a lift. Sure
enough, in about five minutes, up drove a red-
faced farmer, in an old mud-spattered buggy—
very slovenly. Always find slovenliness and good-
nature go together. Says I, "Good morning."
"Good morning," says he. "If you are goin' my
way I'll gie ye a lift." "I'm going to Ballan,"
says I. "I'm just goin' there too." So he
stopped his horse, and I got up, and he drove

away. He was an amusing cuss, but I learnt nothing of B—— from him. Good-natured folks don't notice anything. It's the ill-natured sort that observe and find out things. If there's a black spot on a man's character they'll see it in a brace of shakes and paint it blacker. Nothing escapes that sort. I never knew a jolly detective yet. I'm of the melancholy sort myself.

'We got to Ballan by dinner-time. My friend pulled up to water his horse at a second-rate hotel. A pretty strong whiff of roast pork came round the corner, so I says, "Will you take a snack of something for dinner?" "Thank ye," says he. "I've noticed that the good-natured sort is always ready to eat. They never say no."

'There was a tramp sitting at the table, with a big swag on the form beside him. He looked at me in a suspicious sort of way, and I took stock of him. He must have known me, for the sight of me took away his appetite. Only frighten a man, and if you have to board him, you'll do it cheap. He soon took out his pipe and tobacco, as I expected, for they always smoke when they want to steady their nerves. He then pulled out a white-handled knife and began to cut his tobacco. When he had cut enough he laid down the knife

beside him. Shakespeare says there are "sermons in stones and books in the running brooks;"
and so there are in penknives, if you only know
how to read them. Lor' bless you! I once hanged
a man for murder from what a penknife told me.

'I said to the tramp, "Lend me your knife to
cut my tobacco." He would have hidden it, but
my eye was on him and he saw it was no use.
He handed it over. You remember telling me
that the man I was in search of had taken a knife
from your shop, with J. R. (your boy's initials) on
it. I held the identical knife in my hand: no
mistake about it. There was J. R. on it as plain
as print. I pulled out a pair of darbies that I
always carry in my coat pocket, and I went over to the
tramp. Says I, "I'm a detective. This is a stolen
knife, and if you don't tell me where you got it I'll
handcuff you and take you to the lockup." "Is
that all?" says he. "I got that knife from my
mate." "What is your mate like, and where is
he?" says I. The tramp hesitated a moment, so I
said, "Here goes then," and I shook the darbies.
He got as white as a sheet, and he said, "Well,
McWhilly, I'll make a clean breast." Says I, to
cut a long story short, "What had he got on his
chin?" "Well, McWhilly, you're on the lay. He's

got a mole on his chin." "Anything on the mole?" says I. "Three hairs," says he. "Right," says I. "Where is he? I know, so tell me the truth or you're a gone coon." "He's on Golden Point, third tent from the main road, right hand." "Is that true?" says I. "Yes," says he. I saw he was telling the truth. I said, "I may just warn you; if what you say isn't true, you'll be run in before you go far."

'My good-natured friend had been listening, open-mouthed, to all we had been saying, and he now chimed in:

'"Blest if I didn't think you was a softie. Who'd a thought you was a detective? It'll be a good joke to tell my missus when I get home!"

'"Many thanks for the lift," says I.

'"You're welcome," says he.

'I paid for the dinner and drinks. I was sure of my man now. I was in a hurry to get to Ballarat; I had heard the Ballarat coach would pass the door in a quarter of an hour. I shook hands with my good-natured farmer. He jumped into his buggy, and drove away north, to his farm among the hills. The tramp lay down near the horse-trough, and fell asleep.

'The coach drove up. I held up my hand.

The driver stopped his horses, and I got on the box-seat. We drove away in a cloud of dust. Through the dust I thought I saw the tramp get up and walk away. "If I'm sold after all," thought I, "I'll be down on that fellow."

'We got to Ballarat about eight o'clock. I went straight to Golden Point. I counted one tent, two tents on the right hand from the main road, then I come to a gap.

'"What's become of the tent that was standing here this afternoon?" says I to a man at number two tent.

'"Oh!" says he, "the man that owned that place got a telegram about three hours ago, and he took his tent down in a hurry, and said he was going to Creswick to the rush."

'"Sold!" said I, and I went into the middle of the road and "swore at large."

'I went down to the telegraph office and went in. I knew the operator. I said, "Did a telegram come through from Ballan to a man at the third tent from the main road, Golden Point, this afternoon?"

'"Yes," said he, "and delivered at 4.40."

'"What was in it?" said I.

'He took up the message, which was lying

beside him, and read out, "McWhilly is on the lay. Clear quick."

'I stayed in Ballarat for a week, and I never came across the faintest sign of the man I was in search of. You may as well look for a needle in a stack of hay as look for a man in hiding on the diggings. Bless you, he has only to go down a hole, an' lie close, and the devil himself could not find him! I did my best, as you'll allow. It was all that beastly tramp. I'll take it out of him some day.   'W. McWhilly.'

Jack read the whole of the report, and not one word escaped his eye or his brain. He read, and he understood the meaning and significance of every minute detail. He seemed to feel that every stroke of the detective's pen was engraved in clear-cut lines just under the base of his skull. He could turn his spiritual gaze upon the writing at any time. It was indelibly fixed like a carbon print which the photographer warrants not to fade. He handed the document to the bookseller, and he gave a long-drawn sigh.

'If I had not promised my mother that I would do my best to find uncle, I would almost give up the idea; but I cannot go back now. My mind is made up. Perhaps I will succeed where the detective failed.'

'There is just one point on which I have no information.'

'What is that?' said the bookseller.

'The detective says nothing descriptive about the tramp. I will go and ask him to describe the man. The whole thing is like one of those puzzles you sometimes see. If one of the pieces is missing you can't put it together. If a link is gone the rest of chain may slip through your fingers.'

Jack put on his hat and went to the detective office. McWhilly was just coming out.

'I want to see you,' said Jack. 'Please describe to me the exact appearance of the tramp you saw at Ballan. The man, I mean, who had my knife.'

'What's up, my boy? I've vowed to pay that fellow out.'

Jack told him that he was going to Ballarat to look for the man the bookseller had commissioned him to find, and, as a clue, he wanted a description of the 'tramp.'

'I don't mind telling you, my boy. It isn't professional, mind that, and the man's my game.

I've winged him already, and brought him down. I've only to bag him when I think it's worth my while. I'd hang him, too, to carry out the sportsman idea, if I could; but I wouldn't eat him, hang me if I would! ha! ha!'

'At any rate give me his description,' said Jack.

'All right; don't be impatient, my buck.'

The detective pulled out a fat pocketbook and turned over its pages. At last he opened it wide and read:

'Tramp at Ballan. Five feet six inches high, broken nose, black eyes, tooth missing in front, scar over right eye, dark complexion, black hair, white tuft behind.'

The detective gabbled this off.

'All right,' said Jack; 'I'll make a copy.' He wrote the description in his pocketbook.

'If you ever clap eyes on that fellow,' said the detective, 'he's wanted; send for me.'

Jack went away. He told the bookseller that he had seen the detective. He arranged to be absent for a month. If at the end of that time he could not find his uncle, he was to come back and give up the search.

CHAPTER V

THAT same afternoon Jack was sitting on the box-
seat of the Bendigo coach, in front of Cobb's
booking office. The coachman sat beside him,
with the reins in his hand, a straw in his mouth,
a pink in his buttonhole. The horses tossed their
heads and were impatient to be off. The luggage
was packed, the last passenger had taken his seat.
The coachman shook the reins and cracked his
whip. Away went the horses, as if they had no
intention of pulling up till the end of the first
stage. They suddenly stopped, however, of their
own accord, at the post office, to get the mails.
Two men in scarlet coats were waiting. The
coachman hoisted up the lid of the 'boot' with
his heel. The mailbags were tumbled in, the lid
was shut with a snap, and away the coach went,
rattling over the dry and dusty street. In a few
minutes Elizabeth Street, the backbone of the city,
with all its ribs running east and west, was left

behind. The passengers began to strike matches
on their trousers or soles of their boots; then
hide their head, pipe, and match inside their hats
until they had got their tobacco fairly lit; then
they clapped their hats on their heads; smiled
with satisfaction, as if they had done something
worthy of notice, and began to smoke like chimneys.

Bullock drays, horse teams. butchers' carts,
drays, &c., were left behind; cricketers turned
their heads to see the rolling patch of red rush
past; cottage doors were frames for brown faces,
touzled hair, and inquisitive eyes; children making
dirt pies lifted their smudged faces, and raised a
feeble cheer; dogs rushed after the galloping horses
and barked frantically, as if they were doing a day's
work in three minutes. Yellow grass, wild flowers,
thistles, gorse, post and rail fences, and stunted gum
trees whirled past. Lowing cattle, bleating sheep,
and neighing horses then came upon the scene;
then the smell of manna in the trees, and honey,
laid by in store by the bees in the high, hollow
trunks. The hills began to show in the north, all
purple and gold, and the sun was setting like a ball
of fire, when the coach drew up at Keilor for a
change of horses.

Jack got down from his perch and interviewed

the landlady of the hotel.   He was going to stay at
Keilor for the night.   He wanted to go the same
route the detective had taken.   He thought it was
the right thing to do.   If there was anything to
find out on the way, he could pick it up and use it
in his search.

'Can you let me have a bed for the night?'

'Oh, yes,' said the landlady.   'There's a room
with a spare bed.   It's the only bed that isn't
taken.'

'All right,' said Jack.

He had a wash, and went in to tea.   It was
served in a long room with slab walls and a bark
roof.   The company was as heterogeneous as a bag
of mixed lollies, rough as primitive cave-men, and
armed at all points like a prickly pear.   Every
man had a revolver in his belt and a knife on his
right hip.   They were all diggers, going to or
returning from the gold-fields.   If Jack had
dropped from the clouds he could not have been
more astonished.   He felt rather scared, and his
face showed it.

'Hillo, youngster! where are *you* off to?' said
the man at his right hand, who was shovelling
potatoes and cabbage into his mouth with a horn-
handled knife.

Jack looked at the man, and thought he had seen him before.

'Don't ye know me?' said the man.

'I think I do,' said Jack, 'but where I have seen you I cannot remember.'

'I remember you very well, youngster. I used to bring firewood to your mother's place all last winter.'

'I remember now,' said Jack. 'I never saw you with your hat off, so no wonder I didn't know you.'

'Where are you going to, boy? Are you running away?'

'I'm going to Ballarat,' said Jack, 'partly on business.'

'So am I,' said the man. 'Me and my mate,' pointing with his thumb to the man beside him, 'is going to Ballarat to try our luck. There's precious little firewood wanted now that summer is come; so we are off. I've brought the horse, to carry the tent and our picks and shovels. If you're going our way, you can share the tent with us, and take a bit o' what's going at grub-time.'

Jack liked the man's face. He remembered that his mother had said the woodman was honest, so he replied at once that he would be glad to go with

M

the men if they would let him pay his share. The woodman said, 'All right.'

As they were to start early in the morning they soon wanted to go to bed. To Jack's disgust he found he had to sleep in a room with four beds in it. One bed was already occupied by a stertorous sleeper. He was ruefully looking at the bed which had been pointed out to him as the one he was to sleep in, when to his great joy his friend the woodman popped his head in at the door and said, 'This is my crib, is it? All right.' Seeing Jack, he came in quickly. 'Me and my mate is going to sleep here too. That's lucky. We can wake each other early.'

The woodman's name was Tom, and his mate's Bill. These were the only names Jack ever knew them by.

Jack slept well. He was awakened by feeling himself roughly shaken by Tom.

'Get up, lad. The sun is shining and the birds are singing.'

Jack jumped out of bed, and was soon washed and dressed. He slung his knapsack, which contained a slender kit, over his shoulder. In a few minutes he was standing at the door. Bill brought the horse, which had passed the night in the small paddock attached to the hotel. The tent was packed, also the shovels and picks, and thus laden, the horse waited quietly till the reckoning was paid; then Tom said, 'Gee up,' and away went horse, men, and boy westward, across the plain, their long shadows, like spears, leading the way.

'Do you know the road ?' said Jack.

'Oh, yes,' said Tom. 'Nor'-nor' by west.'

'Is that all you know ?'

'What more does a man want to know ?' said Bill. 'You get your course from the captain, and you've nothing to do but steer. Tom and me came from the Cape once. When it was his turn at the wheel the captain said, 'East.' When it was my turn at the wheel, the mate said 'East.' That's the only course we had in 5,000 miles, and we hit Port Phillip Head as straight as an arrow. On a course of nor'-nor' by west, our old mate, Bill Bo'sun, told us we would hit the main Ballarat road about four bells on the second day out.'

'Well, he knows, I suppose,' said Jack.

'All right,' said Bill, 'he knows. He took the bearings, and kept the log out and home.'

They plodded steadily on till about nine o'clock, when a halt was called for breakfast. Bill unloaded the horse and hobbled him. Then he left him to

browse on the scanty grass. Meanwhile, Tom and
Jack had collected a little dry wood and bark. The
fire was soon kindled. The 'billy' was filled from
a clear pool of water close by. Jack saw a big
bird fly out of a tree, and he went, boy-like, to see
if there was a nest. He climbed up and found a
large one made of sticks and grass. There were
three eggs in it. He put them in his coat pocket,
and came down. When he got to camp he found
the 'billy' had been taken off the fire; a handful of
tea had been thrown in. Tom poured out a pannikin of tea for each. Then he produced some bread
and cold meat. Jack placed the three eggs in the
hot embers to roast. When they had eaten some
bread and meat, he pulled the eggs out of the
ashes with a crooked stick, and gave each of the
men one. He cracked the shell of the other. They
all began to eat them, very gingerly at first. As
the taste was good they went on eating, and did not
stop till every particle was done. In one breath
they declared they had never eaten a better egg.
They were all in high spirits, and much refreshed.
The men had a smoke. Jack lay at full length on
the grass, and thought of what he would do when
he got to Ballarat. He thought of his mother and
Mary, and the burning shame and disgrace of his

and their relationship with the man he was going to find. He was going to find him—no doubt on this subject ever entered his mind now. He had begun the search, and he was going to succeed, with God's blessing. And after he had found him ; what then—happiness or misery ?

He was suddenly aroused from his reverie by Tom calling out ' Pipe all hands.'

He jumped to his feet. The horse was laden, and standing patiently.

' Nor'-nor' west by west,' said Tom, and they all went on in that direction.

' How far will you go to-day ? ' said Jack.

' We mean to anchor for the night at the Merribee river. I would clap on all sail, but this old Dutch-built tub of a horse will only sail three knots an hour. He isn't a clipper, so there's no use cracking on.'

In the early afternoon they entered the main street of Bacchus Marsh.

' We must get some soft tack at the baker's,' said Bill. ' Keep your weather eye open as we sail up the street.'

' There is a baker's shop a little farther on,' said Jack.

' How do you know ? Thought you'd never been here before.'

'A friend of mine told me all about the road to Ballarat, so I know there is a baker's shop a little farther on. There it is, I believe, on the left-hand side.'

'All right—belay! you go in, boy, and get a four-pounder.'

Jack went in and asked the baker's wife, who came in at the tinkle of the bell, for a four-pound loaf.

'We haven't a loaf in the shop,' said the woman. 'We sent the last lot down to the store half-an-hour ago.'

Jack's face fell. They must have bread. To go back to the store was to lose time. He was getting a little foot-sore too, as he had walked further than he had ever walked in his life.

The woman looked at the boy with a wistful eye. Something in his appearance seemed to call up memories of the past. Her eyes suddenly filled with tears. Two or three large drops trickled over, and ran down her cheeks. Jack looked at her in astonishment.

'What is the matter?' he said.

'Oh, my boy! you remind me of my own boy who is dead and gone.' Here the mother gave way, and sobbed as if her heart would break.

'Don't go away,' she said, after she had wiped her eyes. 'I'll bring my husband.'

She went out to the kitchen, and in a few minutes she came back with her husband. She had evidently told him that the boy in the shop reminded her of the son who was dead.

He was in his shirt-sleeves, plentifully sprinkled with flour, a baker's cap on his head, a kindly, rosy face beneath, and soft, tender eyes. He was a Scotchman.

'Let me see ye, ma lad.' He took Jack by the top of his head and chin, and held his face up to the light for two minutes. 'Yes, it's a maist extraordinar likeness, wife! Whar' dey ye come frae, and whar' are ye gaen tae, ma dear boy?'

'Have you got a mother?' said the woman.

'Yes.'

'Well, I envy her. I wish I could keep you all to myself.' She gave him a great hug, and said, 'Oh, my bonny boy! my bonny boy!'

'Rin, gude wife, an' set the best ye hae on the table, an' he'll tak something wi' us. It's jist as if our Willie had come hame after a lang absence. Maybe the gude Lord has sent him this way to ca' upon us to cheer us up like.'

His wife had never taken her eyes off the boy

all this time. She just seemed absorbed in con-
templation. She was trying to make out fresh
resemblances of her dead boy.

Jack was touched by the evident emotion of
the baker and his wife. At last he said, 'I am
sorry I must go. We must get some bread at the
store, I suppose.'

'Ye canna gang the nicht. No, no, ma lad! Ye
canna leave us just the noo. Ye maun eat at our
table, and drink o' our cup, and sleep in Willie's
bed, jist tae please us. Maybe we are entertainin'
an angel unawares. The Lord has sent ye tae us,
just for ae nicht, jist for ae nicht.'

Jack was soft-hearted. The couple clung to
him wistfully. He could not tear himself away.
He explained that he had two friends outside waiting for him, and he really must go.

'No, no, lad! I'll gang oot an' speak tae
them,' said the baker.

He went out and explained the whole matter to
Tom and Bill.

Tom said 'I'm blest!' and Bill said 'I'm
blest!'

The baker sent a boy to the store for bread,
who soon came back with two loaves. He gave
them to Tom and Bill. It was agreed that Jack

was to stay all night at the baker's, and that the
two men were to go on to the Merribee and camp
for the night. The baker promised to drive Jack
to the camping-place by seven o'clock in the
morning.

'Well, I'm blest!' said Tom, 'if this here isn't
the rummest go. Beats Robinson Crusoe an' the
desolate island all to fits. Seems more as if I was
Reuben goin' down into Egypt to buy bread, an'
I was leavin' Benjamin behind. Expect I'll meet
Jacob somewhere, an' he'll say, "Where's Benjamin?"'

The baker hurried Jack into the shop as soon
as Tom and Bill were fairly away.

'Now, my laddie, come ben. It's real kind of
ye, so it is, jist to humour an auld man an' his
wife, because we fancy we see a likeness in ye to
our dear bairn in heevin.'

He took Jack affectionately by the shoulders
and led him to the 'best' room, where the good
wife had spread her snowiest tablecloth, and laid
out an abundant and dainty meal. Everything
was of the very best, and Jack's appetite, which
was very keen by this time, prompted him to
begin. He hung back, however, when he saw that
only one chair was placed at the table. He looked

up inquiringly and said, 'Am I to sit down all alone, Mrs. White?' He knew her name now, for he had slyly glanced at the sign above the door.

'If you could only call me mother, just for one night, it would remind me of my boy,' she said wistfully.

'We've had our denner, boy, and we could na eat a bit; we'll jist be real happy if you'll go on by yoursel.'

The good wife pressed him to begin. Then she went to the end of the table and poured out a cup of tea, with plenty of cream and sugar in it. Jack ate heartily, and drank two or three cups of tea. Then he said, 'Mother, would you please give me another cup?'

At the word 'mother' a tear fell from the woman's eye and hissed on the lid of the teapot for a moment.

'That's the sweetest sound I've heard for a long time. I wish your name was Willie that I might call you by it. It would just be heavenly. You're sitting in Willie's chair and in Willie's place, and I'm a happy woman to-day; but I dread to-morrow when you'll be away. Oh, boy, if you'll only come and see us sometimes, at holidays say, we would look forward to your visits and be just happy when you were with us.'

After a long time, as it seemed to Jack, he finished eating and drinking, and leant back in his chair. He had been suddenly thrust into a very prominent position in this simple household. He felt himself a hero of romance. He had come out to look for adventures, and here he was, suddenly plunged into one he had not bargained for. There was enough for a three-volume novel—sunshine and tears, love and death.

The baker came in from the garden. His eye was moist, and he surreptitiously wiped away a tear. Recollections of his boy had overcome him. The wound was still fresh, and it was inclined to bleed. With a view to changing the subject uppermost in his thoughts he said, 'Dick has come back. He's lying asleep in the summer-house.'

'Who is Dick?' said Jack, well disposed to make a dash through the opening thus presenting itself.

'Dick,' said the baker's wife, 'used to work in the bakehouse. He was very fond of Willie, and would take him out bees'-nesting, fishing, kangarooing, or 'possum hunting. He just loved the boy. He would spend every moment he could with him—play marbles with him, spin tops, fly kites, or anything else Willie fancied. It was quite beautiful to see his devotion. You may guess we will do anything for Dick, although he has been a sore trial since we lost our boy. He just couldn't settle to any work since then, and he has taken up with bad characters, and left us for weeks together. He gets fits of remorse, and comes back, and works faithfully for awhile, and then he says he must go away again, for he cannot endure the place without Willie.'

When Willie's name was mentioned there was a sob preceding the word and a tear following it. It cut to the mother's heart, as the gardener's knife cuts the branch when he prunes it and the sap-tear follows. Tears are the heritage of all living things. If they bring sorrow they also bring joy. Many a mother, through her tears, has seen far into the heavenly city.

The baker was getting perilously near a break-down again. He went to the window and looked out. 'There's Dick,' he said : 'come out and see him.' Jack jumped up and went to the window. He could just see a man, stretched at full length, on a seat in the summer-house.

'I would like a nearer view of Dick,' said Jack.

'Very well,' said the baker. 'Come oot and maybe he'll wake up by-and-by.'

The man and boy went into the garden. The bees were laden with honey, and yellow with pollen. The flowers were shedding their perfume on the lazy afternoon air. The pigeons were cooing on the housetop. Butterflies were flitting from bloom to bloom ; and here, amid this peaceful scene, lay a man, evidently sleeping off a debauch. 'Only man is vile,' says the poet. Jack was just about to repeat the verse, but he thought it would not be kind, so he refrained. Mrs. White came out to them.

The man was lying with his face buried in his hands. His hat had fallen off. He had black hair and there was a white tuft in it. Jack gave a start of surprise. His face became crimson. If he had not held on to a post of the summer-house, he would have probably fallen to the ground. He soon recovered. He thought to himself, 'This is the tramp McWhilly saw at Ballan.'

He turned to the baker and said, 'I am a necromancer or a wizard. I never saw this man before ; I cannot see his face, yet I will describe it. Tell me if I am right.'

'He has a broken nose.'

'Richt,' said the baker.

'Black eyes.'

'Richt again!'

'Scar over right eye.'

'Richt once mair!'

'Tooth missing in front.'

'Maist extraordinar! Have ye seen a photo of 'im?'

'No! I never saw a photo of him, and I never saw the man before the present time. I will tell you more about this man. I see his past life mapped out before me. Once a man came here; a man with a mole on his chin, with three hairs growing on it.'

'Oh, laddie, stop! stop! ye're surely a wizard or a warlock.'

'Let me go on,' said Jack. 'This man with the mole met Dick somehow and somewhere. I cannot see how or where, but I know somehow they did meet. The man with the mole induced Dick to go with him to the diggings—yes! Ballarat—and they became mates. The man with the mole taught Dick to drink, and after he drinks he thinks he sees Willie and he is filled with remorse, and he comes back here to try and get away from evil ways and drink.'

'It's a' true as gospel. Ye maun be an angel
o' licht, for nane ken what ye tauld us but oorsels.'

Jack laughed. 'I could tell you much more, but
this is enough. I would like to speak to Dick when
he awakes. I have something to ask him and
something to say to him. Come into the house.'

Mrs. White had been looking at the boy with rapt
gaze. He must be an uncommon boy. He was no ordinary traveller. He was altogether extraordinary.
Everything he had said and done, in the few hours
she had known him, struck her as being remarkable.

The three went into the house. The baker
and his wife were too astonished to speak. They
were cogitating with themselves as to what manner
of boy this was who was able to describe Dick's
appearance and tell the main points of his life
since Willie's death. Jack was amused at their
evident bewilderment, but he soon began to think
that his rôle of fortune-telling could not be main-
tained if he were to question Dick about his uncle
and get any information out of him worth knowing. He saw that he could only get information
from him through Mr. and Mrs. White. When
this dawned upon him he at once told them that
the man with the mole was his uncle, and how he

had learnt everything he knew about Dick from
the detective who had called at the baker's some
months before.   He told them his whole story.
While telling it they listened with wide eyes and
open mouth.   When he had finished the baker
said :

'You are nae common boy, and you'll be nae
common man.   You mind me o' a story tauld me
by the dominie when I was a boy at schule.   You
see, I had a little Latin, an' a smattering o' Greek.
When I got into the Greek, the dominie tauld us
that, when the great historian Thucydides was a
boy, he was noted for his studiousness.   He would
be aye writin' essays, an' his schulefellows wad
come to him to write theirs.   His schulemaister,
seeing Thucydides' cleverness, said to him ae day,
"Boy, when ye grow up ye'll be nae common man."
Noo, Jack! my wife and me think an uncommon
lot o' ye for comin' oot into the wilds to look for
yer uncle.   It's the maist astonishin' thing we
ever hard tell o'.   Ye'll be nae common man,
I'm thinkin', nae common man ! '

After tea Jack proposed waking Dick, for the
purpose of questioning him about his uncle.

'Leave Dick to me,' said Mrs. White.

The three went to the summer-house.   Mrs.

White shook Dick by the shoulders. He said softly, 'All right, Willie, I'm coming.'

'Just listen to him,' she said.

'It's me! Waken up! I want to speak to you,' said the baker.

Dick opened his eyes and looked round. Seeing the baker, Mrs. White, and Jack, he got off the seat, very unsteadily. He held on to it for a minute, then he staggered away.

'Leave him alone,' said the baker; 'he kens what he's doin'.'

Dick went straight to the pump, and, with a few vigorous strokes of the handle, the water came. He put his head under. In this position he kept the water going for about five minutes. Then he suddenly stopped pumping, and looked round smiling.

'I'm as right as a trivet now, boss.'

'I'm thinkin', Dick, ye've nae enemy but yersel. Puir fellow! Come an' get some tea.'

Mrs. White took Dick away to get the tea. When they were gone Jack said: 'It will be better for me not to be present when you question Dick about my uncle. All I want to know is where he is now, or where he is likely to be found.'

N

'Better so. My wife an' me can manage tae get that oot o' him.'

The baker left Jack in the garden. He went to his wife, who was now giving Dick some tea. He whispered into his wife's ear, 'Ask him where the man with the mole on his chin is.'

'I hope you will never go near the man with the mole on his chin again, Dick.'

'Oh, no fear, missis!

'Where is he now, Dick?'

'Curse him! I never want to hear about him again.'

'Is he on Ballarat?'

'Yes.'

'What part?'

'Pegleg Gully.'

'Have you quarrelled with him?'

'Yes. I believe he's made his pile. Made me drunk; turned me out; was in the lock-up a week.'

After Dick had had his tea, he went off to a little room behind the bakehouse to have another sleep. Mrs. White hurried out and told Jack that his uncle was on Pegleg Gully, Ballarat.

'Many thanks;' said Jack: 'I can never repay you for all your kindness.'

The baker and his wife sat with Jack in the 'best' room till late that night. They had become intensely interested in Jack's family history. They could not speak of anything else.

'It just bangs a'. Just as absorbing as Josephus' account o' the takin' o' Jeroosalem,' said the baker.

Mrs. White showed Jack his bedroom, which had been Willie's. Everything was scrupulously neat and clean. The baker called out, 'I'll waken ye at half-past five.'

Jack had no sooner laid his head on the pillow than he fell fast asleep. It had been a most exciting day, crowded with incident. Towards morning he began to dream. He thought his uncle was breaking into the room, and that he had got out of bed to prevent him. All at once he imagined the window fell in with a crash—the glass broke in a thousand fragments around him. He grasped his uncle, and held him tight. Then he thought they struggled and fought on the floor for hours, till he was left stunned and bleeding. When he awoke, with a start, he found he had fallen out of bed and that he was grasping a pillow. He slowly picked himself up and went to the window. There was no catch; every pane was whole. Morning was breaking: a pale rosy flush was spreading in the

east : the morning star was getting faint and dim.
The swallows began to twitter in their nests and
the Australian nightingale was finishing his song.
Jack crept into bed ; sleep had departed, and could
not be wooed back again.   The baker came to the
door about half-past five and knocked.

'Get up, Jack,' he called ; 'ye mind I promised
ye wad be at the Merribee by seeven o' the clock.'

Jack tumbled out of bed and dressed himself
quickly.   He very soon threw his window up and
opened the door.   Mrs. White was waiting for him.
She gave him a kiss, and hoped he had slept well.
Then she led him to the breakfast-table in the next
room.   The baker came hurrying in, and shook
hands with Jack.   He clapped him on the back and
told him that he looked fresh as hot rolls, and
brown as a loaf just drawn from the oven.   They
then sat down, and made a hearty breakfast.

The tramp of a horse's hoofs and the grating of
wheels came very distinctly on the still morning
air.   The baker ran out, and immediately ran in
again.   He popped his head in at the door and
called, 'All aboord.'   Jack jumped up, so did Mrs.
White, and she clung to the boy for a moment.
Then she said, 'Promise me faithfully that you'll
come back soon, for I'll never be happy till ;you

come again.' Jack promised, and the good woman followed him to the door. A horse and buggy were standing all ready for the journey. The baker was in his seat, with the reins in one hand, the whip in the other. With a final kiss Mrs. White let Jack go. He jumped up; White said 'Gee up,' and they were off. Jack turned round and took off his hat. There stood Mrs. White, with a tear in her eye, but a smile on her face. Thus she remained till a bend of the road hid the boy from her sight. The light went out of her eyes and the smile from her face. She went slowly into the house, and she said softly to herself, 'I know he will come again.'

The horse went on; he was accustomed to go his daily rounds with bread. The first house he came to he stopped, and would not proceed till the baker pretended to take a basket, with an imaginary loaf, and go in at the cottage gate, giving the customary bang. In a minute he came back and got up to his seat. The horse went on quite satisfied. The same ceremony had to be gone through at every house. Fortunately they were few and far between, so there was not much time lost, and there were no cross roads till the top of the hill was reached. Then the horse wanted to go to the right as usual, but the baker's patience was exhausted by

this time. He said, 'Drat ye! tak that,' and he
gave the beast a sharp cut over the right flank.
The horse looked round in astonishment. He had
never been so treated before.

'Weel noo, I couldna help it. This conduct o'
yours is jist too much for a saunt.'

He jumped down, and went to the beast's head
and patted it, and whispered to it in endearing
fashion. Jack thought he heard him say, 'I am
very sorry, so I am ; I beg your pardon.' He led
the horse down the hill a hundred yards or so, then
he got up to his seat again and took the reins out
of Jack's hands.

'That beast's as forgivin' as the best Christian
amang us.'

At the foot of the hill they came to the Merribee
river, and crossed it at the ford. About a stone's-
throw up the stream they saw Tom and Bill's tent.
Jack 'cooeed.' Tom peeped out at the tent door
and said, 'Well, Benjamin, has Joseph let ye go ? '

The baker drew up at the tent. He pulled
out a basket from under the seat, and took from it
a small flour bag, which he handed to Jack.

'Jist a few things from my wife, which she
tauld me no to forget.'

'Oh, thank you,' said Jack. 'I shall never forget the kindness you and she have shown me.'

'My boy, don't you forget us. She'll be terrible grieved if ye don't come to see us soon.'

'I promise you I'll come soon. I will not forget, I assure you.'

'That's a good boy. Be sure.'

Here the baker hesitated, and began to stammer. He could not say another word. He waved his hand, turned the horse's head homewards, and went slowly on his way. Jack watched him cross the ford and go up the steep hill. He never looked back once.

Jack handed the bag to Tom, and told him to open it. He did so. The first thing he saw was a little parcel tied to the mouth of the bag. He opened it, and said 'I'm blest!' He slapped his thigh and laughed.

'What's the matter?' said Jack.

'Look here,' said Tom. He held up a coin. 'This is the identical shilling I gave the baker last night for the bread.'

'No!' said Jack.

'Yes! Benjamin; it's the money in the sack's mouth. It's Joseph's doing. I didn't think he would have let you out of Egypt. Ha! ha!'

He pulled out some nice tartlets and cakes, a pot of jam, a jar of ginger, a cooked knuckle of ham, and some bread.

' Enough for a week. We're in luck an' no mistake,' said Bill.

The men sat down and took a good square meal. When they had eaten their fill they struck the tent, rolled it up, and packed it on the horse, also the spades and picks. They slung the bag of bread, cakes, &c., on top. Then they wended their way along the lush flats. Dewdrops sparkled on every blade of grass, white cockatoos chattered in the trees at a respectful distance, tree flies dinned their discordant song into unwilling ears, lizards, in silver and green, darted here and there, kingfishers flashed with jewelled wing, bees hummed and beetles droned in the still morning air. It was a peaceful and quiet spot. Jack walked on with springy gait, enjoying everything, and the two men, who were little used to such scenes, could not help seeing that Nature was in one of her most charming moods.

They made good headway, and only halted about noon for a quarter of an hour, without unlading the horse. They ate some bread and ham, also some tartlets and cakes, which were too good

to neglect, and drank of the crystal stream that
came fresh from the mountains and flowed across
their path.

In the afternoon they got into a broad, well-
defined road, full of bullock dray ruts. Horse and
cattle teams were passed—they were nearly all
going west. Diggers in twos and threes were
trudging along. An occasional cart made its appearance, laden with scant household stuff, a
woman and children sitting on top. A mob of
sheep in a cloud of dust, with a yelping dog
behind, were going to market and death ; and fresh
mounds of yellow clay and gravel, on each side of
the road, betokening the outskirts of the famous
Ballarat diggings, were coming thick and plentiful.

The signs were plain and clear. There was no
need to say, ' This is Ballarat.' Fortunes had been
made here ; storekeepers had become rich, diggers
had risen in the morning without a shilling, and,
by night, were worth thousands of pounds.

CHAPTER VI

JACK had been advised by McWhilly, the detective,
to go straight to the Eldorado Hotel, which, he
said, was a quiet house, kept by a countrywoman
of his own who would make Jack comfortable and
advise him what to do. He kept a sharp eye on
each side of the road for the hotel he was in quest
of. He told Tom and Bill he must leave them
soon, as he had to dig at the Eldorado, while they
were going to live in White Horse Gully, where a
friend of theirs had been doing well for some weeks.
By dint of inquiries here and there, they learnt
that the Eldorado was on the main road, about
half a mile farther on. At last it hove in sight,
and Jack called a halt. He pulled out his purse,
with a shy sort of manner, as if he did not quite
approve of what he was doing.

'No, no, Benjamin, none o' that!' said Tom.
'Why, we've been living in clover ever since we met
you.'

'Well,' said Jack, 'you must take a glass of beer.'

' We'll take a glass of beer,' said Bill.

They tethered the horse to a hitching post, and the three went into the bar. They had the beer, shook hands with Jack, and went their way.

Mrs. McWhae, the landlady, a rosy-cheeked, bustling, breezy personage, now came forward and held out her hand. Jack took it and was going to give it a mild shake. It was grasped by Mrs. McWhae, and shaken heartily up and down, as a pump-handle is worked. When it was let go, Jack put it in his pocket, out of harm's way. He was afraid it would be seized upon next by the burly digger who stood by him, and be bruised and mangled in his horny grip. He had some doubts, too, of the barmaid, who was about to hold out her hand also, but drew back just in time when she saw Jack's hand disappear.

Mrs. McWhae said, 'I've been on the look-out for ye a' the efternoon. Maister McWhilly writ me a letter to say ye were comin', an' I'm gled to see ye. The diggins is an unco' place for a callant like ye are. But we'll mak ye at hame.'

She showed him a little room upstairs, at the back of the house, far removed from the noise of the bar and the rattle of the billiard balls. Here, she thought, he would be able to sleep in peace. The bed was a marvel of spotless white curtains and counterpane. The room was a symphony. Window-curtains, toilet-table cover, antimacassars and towels were pure and snowy. The window was wide open. Lavender was in the air.

After a good wash the boy felt refreshed. He lay down on the bed for half an hour to rest, then he got up and went down stairs. He found Mrs. McWhae in a cosy parlour off the bar.

'I had no idea,' said Jack, 'that Mr. McWhilly would write to you and tell you I was coming. He just told me to introduce myself to you, and mention his name.'

'I would do anything for Wullie McWhilly. I've kent him ever since I was a bit lassie, an' we hae been gude freends a' oor life.'

Jack felt at home at once with this kind, motherly woman. He told her the same night as much as he chose to tell of his reasons for coming to Ballarat. He even described the man he was looking for, not imagining for a moment that Mrs. McWhae would ever be able to help him in the search. She put her chin in her left hand for a minute and went into a brown study; then she looked up with a smile.

'Did McWhilly ever look for this man on Ballarat ? '

'Yes ; some time ago.'

'McWhilly's a fule! Thae men bodies hae naé mair gumption in their heids than us women bodies has in oor wee fingers. Wad ye believe it, he sat here, ae nicht, an' talked at lairge about extraordinary marks on folks' faces, sich as strawberry stains an' warts, an' that kind o' thing. If he'd just spoken plain an' clear about moles, an' three hairs growing oot o' ae particular ane, on a man's chin, I could hae put him on his man, for I kend whar he was hidin'. He was jist hidin' in oor stable, under the vera nose o' Wullie McWhilly. I would na hae tauld Wullie though, if it wad hae done the puir man ony harm. No! no! I'm nae that sort!'

She knew nothing now of the man; he had disappeared. He had not been seen near her house for months. His was a remarkable face, and once seen was not easily forgotten. She had often seen him, and knew him well. There were rumours that he had struck a rich patch somewhere, and that he and his mate had quarrelled;

some said he had cheated his mate, some said he had half killed him, and some that he was killed· outright and buried in a deserted shaft. The man was not liked, and was known to be a rogue.

All this and much more Jack learned the same night. All was vague—nothing definite. Someone had seen the man, but he could not remember where. Someone had seen a man who had told him that a friend of his had seen him in Pegleg Gully. This was months ago, and he might be gone now to other 'rushes.' He picked up this information in scraps and shreds, here a little and there a little.

He began to haunt Pegleg Gully. He was there before the sun was up. He wandered up and down it almost every morning for an hour or two, and then he would go to the hotel for breakfast. About twelve o'clock he would be at the gully again, narrowly watching the diggers as they came up from their workings to eat their dinner in the sunlight. He scanned them carefully when they were resuming work. He would be there in the evening again when the men came up for the day.

He had explored the gully with great care. There was no sign : he could hear nothing of the man. Some days had been spent in fruitless effort. If he could only get on his track he would follow it with bloodhound tenacity. If he could only feel sure that he was in the neighbourhood, he would never leave it until he had found him, and said, 'Uncle, I am Jack; I have come to take you home.'

One evening he was just about to give up the search for the day, and was turning down a slight depression that ran off from the main lead. He had not gone far when he saw a small weather-worn tent, a considerable distance from the others. He was sure he had not come this way before, and he thought he had never seen this tent. He went slowly on, with bent head, for he was tired and dejected. He was getting down-hearted. All at once he saw something at his feet. He stooped down to examine it. It was a discoloured pen-knife that had been lying in the dust and mud for some time. The blades were rusty. The handle was encrusted with a thin layer of dirt. He took it up in his hand and rubbed the dry earth off. There was just light enough now to see that there were letters cut on it. There were two. One was a J and the other R. He gave a great start. The initials were his, and the knife was the one his uncle had taken from the shop, and the same that

McWhilly found with Dick. Dick had been here since then, that was clear, and the information he had given of the whereabouts of his uncle was correct. This was also clear. The proof was in his hand. He held the end of the thread and he was going to unravel the tangled skein. The search was getting warm. The quarry could not be far off. When his pulse was a little quieter and his heart beating less fiercely, he put the knife in his pocket. It was nearly dark, so he retraced his steps, went up the gully, and went back to the hotel.

He went to bed, but not to sleep. He tossed about and 'counted the weary hours.' He felt he was on the eve of discovery. The knife had returned to him after many days. 'From small beginnings great events arise.' The acorn does not know it is the mother of navies, thundering out death and deciding the fate of nations. The coral insect does not know it is the greatest builder in the world. The little stone did not know it was going to lay a giant low and scatter the Philistines. When Cortes, and all his men, 'gazed at the Pacific with a wild surmise,' they did not see the commerce wafted from every clime. When Watt saw the steam from the kettle, he did not hear the throb of the engine in every land. When Gutenberg set up his newly invented types, he did not see knowledge spreading over the earth. When Wheatstone played with electricity he did not know he was girdling the globe. When Jack left his knife on the counter of the shop he did not suspect what an important part it was going to play in this history.

He got up in the morning unrefreshed: in body tired; in mind, clear as to what he was going to do. He dressed quickly and went downstairs on tiptoe. He let himself out by the back door, where Boots was groaning and grunting over fifty pairs. He went down the main street, and out into the country, steering straight for Pegleg. There was no stir or movement anywhere. No blue smoke curled from the chimneys; the birds had not begun to sing. The sleeping dogs would not stir, or wag their tongue or tail.

He went round by the back of the gully, and slid down the grassy bank to the spot where he had found the knife. Then he took a good survey around. The nearest tent was the weather-beaten one he had seen the night before. He went close up to it; there was no dog keeping watch at the door; there was no sound within. He stood

O

listening for some time, when suddenly a deep groan came from the tent. It was so eerie in this lonely spot, and so full of misery, he could not help lifting the door-flap and peeping in. A man, half naked, lay on a miserable stretcher formed of saplings and old bags. He was tossing restlessly, and sawing the air with his skinny arms and clenched fists. His eyes were wild and glittering; his hair was matted.

' Water! water! ' he cried.

Jack ran in and took up a pannikin and looked for water. There was not a drop in the tent. He rushed out, and searched in the neighbourhood, but could not find any. He remembered seeing a little spring oozing out of the ground at the foot of the gully. He ran to it and filled the pannikin, and slowly walked back, afraid to spill a drop. How long he had been away he could not tell, but it seemed to him to have been an age. He went into the tent, and took the man round the neck with his right arm and raised his head. With the left he held the pannikin to his lips. The man drank every drop, and called for more. Jack searched about for a bucket; at last he found one under the bed, which he took and went again to the spring and filled it by means of the pannikin.

When he got back to the tent, the gully was showing signs of life. Wood-chopping was going on,
and a few fires were being lit.

Jack filled the pannikin again, and put it to
the man's lips. He drank as before. When he
had finished it he lay down and shut his eyes,
and seemed to fall asleep.

A great awe fell on the boy. He was all alone
with a man who was very unwell—gaunt and
wasted with a consuming fever. He had lain here
perhaps for days, all alone, without a soul to care
for him—to raise his head, or to give him a drink
of water. The place had a neglected look. Empty
gin-bottles were the principal feature. It was the
home of a drunkard. Jack looked at the man
long and earnestly. His face seemed to recall
some memory of the past; but the key was lost,
and the lock could not be forced to reveal the
secret. The beard was short but thick, and apparently of only a few weeks' growth. The blood-
less skin lay over the cheeks like parchment, but
running along under the pallor lay a network of
veins of a pattern he had seen before; but where?
That was the question, and he asked it again and
again, but got no answer. All at once the answer came flashing into his brain, ' *This is the*

man.' With his finger and thumb he pressed back
the hairs of the beard from the chin : there was
the mole with the three hairs.

His uncle lay before him. The long-lost man
was found at last. Fortune had favoured him.
The first thing he must do is to get a doctor, and
thât speedily. The nearest one he knew of lived
near the camp. He could not leave the man now.
He must seek help. He saw a boy gathering chips
and bark a few hundreds of yards away, so he
called to him. The boy looked up inquiringly.
Jack beckoned frantically. The boy threw down
his armful of chips with visions of a snake or an
opossum. When he had got near enough Jack
called out, 'Run for a doctor. There is a sick
man here. If you bring a doctor in half-an-hour
I'll give you five shillings.'

The boy ran off as quickly as his legs would
carry him, and he did not flag in his pace till
he got to the doctor's door. He rapped loud and
long. The doctor came. The boy was out of
breath, but he managed to stammer the message
that a man was sick down at Pegleg, and the
doctor was to come at once.

'Who's to pay me ? ' said the doctor.

'There's a chap there who's got plenty of

money. He promised me five shillings for coming.'

The doctor pondered a moment. Then he said, 'I'll get my hat and stick, and go with you.'

He came soon, and the boy led the way. The doctor was a big, sallow, heavy man, with a snub nose. Not much sentiment about him, but of the rough and ready sort. The boy went on with nimble foot. He was impatient for the fingering of the five shillings, and the spending of them.

The doctor followed, puffing and blowing. 'Look here,' he said, 'if you don't slacken your pace I'll give you a dose of jalap.'

The boy did not know what this might mean, but there was no mistaking the tone in which it was said. The doctor had a stick with which he could give him a dose of another sort, so he slackened his pace and went slower.

'Down this way,' said the boy.

The two descended the bank and were soon at the tent. Jack, hearing voices, came out to meet them. He dropped five shillings into the boy's outstretched hand, and led the doctor in.

After a careful examination of the patient he turned round. 'Typhus—bad case—can't live.'

'What shall I do?' said Jack; 'he's my uncle;

save his life, doctor. Don't spare your time or
expense. Do you think he should go to the
hospital, or should I get a nurse for him?'

'If you move him he'll die on the road. I'll
send a nurse if I can, but I'm afraid there is not
one to be had.' He sat down and wrote a prescription on a leaf of his pocketbook.

'I cannot leave him,' said Jack. 'If it would
not be too much, would you call at the chemist's
and ask him to send the medicine quickly?'

'I'll come again at twelve. My fee is a guinea
a visit.'

Jack dropped a sovereign and a shilling into
the big hand, whose fingers played around them
for a moment like the feelers of an octopus, and
then put them into a pocket.

The chemist's boy came in due course. Jack
detained him till he had opened the parcel. It
contained a bottle with a mixture in it. The
directions were 'a tablespoonful to be taken every
three hours.' There was not a tablespoon in the
tent, nor a glass to put the medicine in. What
was to be done? He would scribble a note on a
scrap of paper and ask the boy to take it to Mrs.
McWhae.

'If you leave this note at the Eldorado, and

bring Mrs. McWhae here in an hour, I'll give you five shillings.'

'Done!' said the boy.

Within the hour Mrs. McWhae and the boy arrived. He was carrying a basket. She went straight into the tent, and said, 'My puir boy, to be left a' yer lane wi' a man doon wi' the fever. That'll never do, never!'

She moved about, putting things in their places. She opened the basket and took out a tumbler and spoon. She then poured out the medicine in the prescribed quantity, and put it in the tumbler. Jack held the man's head up, and she poured the mixture down his throat. Then he lay quiet again and began to mutter and talk in an incoherent way. Then he rolled his eyes in frenzy, and raved and scolded in impotent rage. Then he would lie still for a few minutes, utterly exhausted, just to break out again worse than before. His pulse was throbbing at high pressure, his skin was burning, his tongue was dry, and his eyes were blazing.

Mrs. McWhae sent Jack to the hotel for a small tent, a feather pillow, and a few other things. He walked away rapidly and soon reached the place. He got a cab and put the things in quickly, and caused the man to drive as rapidly as he could.

When he reached the tent he found Mrs. McWhae at the door.

'He's worse,' she said. 'He's ravin' aboot gold. He asked me to bring his sister an' his bairns; he said he wanted to kiss them before he dees.'

'Poor uncle! poor uncle! If I only could do anything for you!' said Jack, ready to cry. He thought of his mother and Mary, and the grief this would bring to them.

Mrs. McWhae quietly slipped the soft feather pillow under the sick man's head. This seemed to give him a little ease for a time; then he shrieked and moaned and tossed about violently, and after a paroxysm sank back in a profuse perspiration.

'Puir man! puir man!'

Mrs. McWhae had brought a little chicken and bread in the basket for Jack. She pressed him to take some. To please her he sat down in the open air, and tried to force himself to eat, but he was unable to swallow a morsel. In the meantime Mrs. McWhae had unrolled the tent and bedding Jack had brought; he came to help her. They soon got the tent put up, and the bedding was spread in a corner on the grass.

'Ye see, you an' me maun keep watch an'

watch, time aboot. It will never do to leave him for lang at a time.'

When night came on Jack insisted on Mrs. McWhae lying down in the newly erected tent, while he kept watch with the sick man. He was to call her if necessary. She went and lay down, hoping to sleep, and she called out ' Wauken me at twelve.'

Jack lighted a candle, and sat down on a box. He watched the patient's every movement, and noted every change. When the time came he gave him the medicine. The man was in a furious delirium about nine o'clock, and he raved at imaginary people who were trying to steal his gold. Suddenly he became quiet; he opened his eyes, and stared at Jack. He said slowly, and very distinctly :—

' Yes, dear wife, I'm coming to you soon. I know I have been bad, but I want to see the children first, I don't know why; I have not seen them since morning. Little Mary and Willie love me, and I love them. I'll leave them all my money. I'm rich now.' He lay with his eyes closed, then he opened them and stared at Jack.

' Who are you? Are you Willie?'

' No, I'm Jack Reeveley, your nephew. You have been unwell, and I have come to nurse you.

When you are better we will go away from here, and you will see Mary and Willie.'

'Yes, Jack, you are like your father, but you have your mother's eyes. I remember now, I have seen you often in my dreams. I was fighting with you last night. Oh, it was a terrible fight: you were going to steal my gold, but you'll never find it—it's hidden, do you hear? No, I haven't got any; not a grain. Very poor—very poor. Go away, and never come near me. You'll never get anything out of me. Go away, go away!'

Another fit of frenzy was coming on. He raved and shouted and roared. He tried to rise, but Jack forced him down again. He was weak as an infant. Then he was still and quiet; his mind was dwelling on the past. He whispered, 'Mary and Willie—come here. That's right. I've got my hands on your heads. I'm happy now. You are to get all my gold. It's hidden under my bed; dig for it; it is deep. Mary, be kind to Willie; Willie, love your sister.'

Here he gave a deep sigh, and said, 'What am I saying? No, no! I've got no gold, do you hear? Not an ounce. What a fool I am! Work for gold, and give it away!'

About midnight there was a change in the

patient. He asked for a drink of water; Jack gave it to him.

'I'm better now; I'll be all right in a day or two. Who are you? I remember. You are Jack Reeveley, you said. I know you now, you were always a good boy. Be kind to Mary and Willie. I've tried to be good for some weeks now, and I have been working like a horse in my claim, night and day, and all for Mary and Willie. Tell them that —yes, tell them that I was going back to them. Yes, I made a vow to God, and He was trying to help me to say 'Our Father,' but the words would stick in my throat, for I had not been a son to Him for many a long day. I'm bitterly sorry now, but it's too late. Pray for me, Jack; pray for me. What's this?'

He put out his hand. 'Yes, wife, I am coming.'

Jack saw that he was sinking fast. He ran and wakened Mrs. McWhae, who came rushing in. When she saw the patient she shook her head. 'It's a' up wi' him.'

He opened his eyes. 'Are you Mrs. McWhae, of the Eldorado? Do I owe you any money? No! that's right. If I do, Jack will pay you.'

'My puir man! You don't owe me onything.

Hae ye made your peace wi' yer Faither in
Heaven ? '

'I have just been asking Him to forgive me, and
He said nothing, but He looked lovingly at me.   I
think He is coming for me soon.   If He comes, I'll
take it as a token.   But I'm afraid, I'm afraid,
He'll never come for me.'

He fell back with a groan.   Mrs. McWhae
thought he was gone.   He opened his eyes again,
and whispered, 'He is coming.'   A smile spread
over his face ; he was dead.

Jack cried a little.   He was thankful that he
had been with his uncle, and that he had been able
to nurse him in his last moments ; he thought now
of his mother, and Mary, and how he would break
the news to them.

Jack told Mrs. McWhae what the dead man had
said about gold, and suggested that it might be well
to dig under the bed.

'If he ever had any gold he never would have
rested till he had spent every penny o't.'

'I think there was something in what he said,
so I must dig after the funeral.'

In the morning Jack went to the doctor.   He
was in bed, and just recovering from a drinking
bout.   When he got the guinea from Jack the day

before, he had kept his promise so far as calling at the chemist's with the prescription; but the next house he came to was a hotel, and he could not pass it with money in his pocket. He went in, and did not come out till night; then he reeled home and went to bed.

'I did not go again at twelve as I said I would. What was the good? I suppose the man's dead.'

'Yes,' said Jack, 'and I want a certificate.'

'All right,' said the doctor. 'My charge for a certificate is two guineas—cash in advance—fork out.'

Jack handed him two guineas. Then he asked the boy to reach him pen, ink, and paper, which, having disposed around him on the bed, he wrote the certificate. Then he flung himself about, and spilled the ink over the counterpane. Jack opened the door and went away in disgust. He went straight to the undertaker's shop, and gave orders for immediate burial. Then he returned to the tent and Mrs. McWhae.

They both sat down in the open air waiting for the undertaker. They were in the vicinity of death, and they spoke in whispers. The woman was touched with the pity of humanity that is always ready to spring up in the feminine breast at

such a time.   She felt for this boy too, who
had been recommended to her care by Willie
McWhilly, her old friend.   She could not leave him
while the corpse was above ground, and she would
accompany him to the grave and see the last rites.

The undertaker made his appearance in the
afternoon. He and his man did all that was
necessary. The coffin was passed into the hearse;
Mrs. McWhae and Jack went into the coach, and
the two vehicles rapidly drove away. The unwonted
sight in Pegleg caused a mild stir. The men were,
with one or two exceptions, down below, and hard
at work. Old Dan Riley, who was the original
prospector in the gully, was rheumatic to-day, and
he was sitting outside his tent door, sunning himself.

‘ I believe it’s the ould bloke,’ he said to Bridget,
his wife.

‘ He wasn’t a bad crayture after all,’ said Bridget.
‘ He wanst met our Mary coming from school, an’
axed her name. When she said it was Mary, he
told her, so he did, that he had wanst a little girl
named Mary, an’ he patted her on the head, so he
did, an’ gave her a shillin’.’

‘ He was a bitter bad one,’ said Dan.

‘ Whist, Dan, sure the poor man’s dead now.

An' if he called his gurl Mary, after the blessed Vargin, sure his sins may be forgiven him.'

'The blessed Vargin wouldn't touch him with a red-hot poker, so she wouldn't,' said Dan.

'How's that, ye ould backbiter ?'

'Becaze when Father O'Moriarty axed him for a shilling to help bury poor Tim Dooley, he tould him to go to blazes.'

'Sure an' isn't he dead ? he may have repinted av' it.'

'He culdn't do it—that's a sin that has no place for repintance.'

'Well! well!' said Bridget, 'I'm sorry for the poor man.'

'You don't mean to tell me it's the owd fellow as lived in the shatteridan place over there ?' said a burly man who had just come up from a claim close by.

'He was a mighty close-fishted ould rip,' said Dan.

'Whist, Dan! Whist!' said Bridget.

'He worn't that, anyway, Dan, for he sent me out five shillings for going up to the camp for the doctor,' said the boy who went the message.

The poor man was dead and buried. Where did he lift up his eyes ? We know not. The priest had stood at the open grave and said :—' Man that is born of a woman hath but a short time to live, and is full of misery. He cometh up, and is cut down like a flower ; he fleeth as it were a shadow, and never continueth in one stay.

'Ashes to ashes : dust to dust.'

Mrs. McWhae and Jack came back before dark with the spring cart from the hotel. She wielded the reins and handled the whip ; they wanted no third person. Jack went into the tent and moved the stretcher aside. Then with his uncle's pick and shovel he dug in the place where the ground had been disturbed. About a foot below the surface he came upon something hard. It was a tin box, without a lock. He lifted the lid ; the box was full of gold. He called Mrs. McWhae. She went in. When she saw the gold, she raised her hands in astonishment, and exclaimed, ' Three thousand ounces if there's a pennyweight.'

Jack ran and got a black bag from the spring cart. He took it in and filled it ; Mrs. McWhae filled her hand-bag. Then the boy was able to lift the tin box. In this way they were able to carry all the gold to the cart. They then drove to the hotel. They put the cart in a stout shed and locked the door. By this time they were both thoroughly exhausted. Jack crept up to bed. Mrs. McWhae went into her parlour and counted the money received during her absence. After locking it up she also sought her bed.

In the morning Mrs. McWhae and Jack harnessed the horse and drove to the Government offices, where they deposited the gold. It weighed 3,211 oz. 4 dwts. It was consigned to the Bank of Australasia, to the credit of John Blenheim, Esq., Bookseller, Bourke Street, Melbourne.

That same night Jack climbed to the box-seat of the Geelong coach. He had taken an affectionate farewell of Mrs. McWhae. He told her he would never forget her and all the kindness she had shown him. He reached Geelong in the early morning, and went to Mac's hotel, where he got breakfast. About ten o'clock he boarded the steamer, which lay at the wharf, all ready to sail. In a few minutes the captain called out, ' Go ahead ! ' and the vessel ploughed her way along the peaceful waters of Corio Bay, past Station Peak, Point Cooke, and Williamstown. Then the Yarra's course was safely negotiated and the Queen's Wharf was reached.

His mother and the bookseller were waiting for him in the crowd, and he was clasped in his mother's arms in spite of onlookers. On the way home he

P

filled in the detail of his adventures, praising his
uncle where he could, for his mother's sake.   It
was arranged that the bookseller was to invest the
proceeds of the gold for the benefit of Mary and
Willie, the children of the dead man, and that they
should never be told of the evil nature of their
father's life ; but that, in some after time, his
loving messages in his last moments should be
made known to them, and that he had left them all
his money.

When McWhilly heard that Jack had discovered
his uncle when he, the trained detective, had failed,
he merely said, ' Some folks are born to luck, others
deserve it.'   Jack gave all the credit to Mrs.
McWhae.   'That woman's worth her weight in
gold,' said the detective.   'She'll be Mrs. McWhilly
some day, mark my words ! '

McWhilly was in Ballarat in a week's time ;
had popped the question, been accepted, and
married within the shortest possible time.   Jack
was 'best man.'   On the wedding morning he
clasped on the bride's wrist the most valuable
bracelet ever seen in Ballarat.

At the first opportunity Jack paid a visit to the
worthy baker and his wife.   They overwhelmed
him with kindness.

Dick never wandered away again. He worked hard in the service of Mr. White, and when the latter retired from business, he succeeded to it, and became a substantial and prosperous man.

It remains only to say that Jack and his cousin Mary were married in a few years. A lovelier bride, or a handsomer bridegroom, was never seen in St. Peter's Church.

A BUSH ADVENTURE

My duties had been very arduous and harassing during the summer of 1854, and my health was suffering in consequence. Following the advice of my medical man, I readily obtained a month's leave of absence, and determined to take an excursion to the residence of a relative, who had a station in the neighbourhood of the Werribee River, where I hoped to recruit my failing health.

I presented myself one fine morning at the Hobson's Bay Railway Station, and secured a through ticket for Williamstown. There were lucky diggers with immense hirsute appendages, burly squatters who owned many a rood, and merchants who were so much accustomed to figures that calculation could be seen in their eyes. There were comfortable fathers of families who dragged along youthful and troublesome charges, nervous mammas full of bother and anxiety, and nurse-girls with bandboxes and crying evils—all bustling off to secure

their seats.   The bell began to ring, porters were
hurry-scurrying up and down the wooden plat-
form, guards were bawling and shouting, and slam-
ming doors and locking them.

The engine was snorting and whistling impatiently; all was wildness and confusion for a few
seconds, when, as if by magic, stillness reigned.
The motley throng had vanished. The guards were
dumb; the porters folded their arms; the engine
whistled shrill, and away we went—over the bridge,
—past the terror-stricken pigs, the bewildered
cattle, and the yelping curs,—past the sign-posts
to the ferries, each purporting to point out the
shortest way,—past the vessels in the river, the
viaduct, and Emerald Hill, and in a twinkling we
thundered up to the Sandridge station.   The
guards unlocked the doors, and another bustling
scene commenced.   Most of the passengers were
bound for England, and went on board a special
steamer which was to convey them to one of the
favourite 'Black Ball' liners, then on the eve of sailing.   A few straggled off towards Sandridge, and a
few, along with myself, went on board the steamer
which ploughed its way across the Bay to Williamstown in a few minutes.

I had sent a few necessaries on before me by the

mail cart, and, as the day was fine, I suddenly determined to walk over the plains, instead of riding, as
I had intended. I had my drawing materials with
me, with which I purposed to make sketches of the
scenery as I went along. I had also a stout
walking-stick to help me on, and a few biscuits for
the inner man. As I had only to walk about fifteen
miles, I sauntered along slowly. I reached the
crossing-place, on the Tea-Tree Creek, about mid-
day, and made a sketch of the remarkable volcanic
boulders which lay scattered along the creek. I
then struck through a fine belt of timber, and the
open plain, until I came to the Skeleton Waterholes,
which I crossed, and then went on my way towards
the Geelong road. I had not proceeded far, when
a fine view of Station Peak presented itself, with
the Pentland Hills in the distance. I sat down to
sketch the lovely scene. In the foreground waved
the tall kangaroo grass; a little further on was
some beautiful rising ground; further still, steeped
in purple, were 'Woolamanta,' or Station Peak,
and the Yowangs; and in the extreme distance
'Myrniong,' or Mount Blackwood, reared its sable
brow.

I sat down full of enthusiasm, and was just
giving a few finishing touches, when—horror of

horrors—I looked behind, and there, within a hundred yards of me, and coming on full tilt, were two or three hundred of the fiercest cattle I had ever seen. Their eyes were glaring with rage, and they stamped on the ground and snorted in anything but an agreeable manner. Their intentions might have been peaceable enough, but I did not like their looks at all. What was I to do? If I remained where I was, I should be trampled on and gored by the infuriated beasts. I jumped to my feet, shouted, and brandished my stick, but to no purpose—on they came—the very ground shook, and so did I. There was nothing for it but to run, and there was no shelter within miles, with the exception of a small, solitary, stunted tree, about a hundred yards off. Towards it I ran at the top of my speed, shouting as I went; but I had hardly time to reach it before they were on me. The tree was only a few feet high, and had not a branch which would support me, so I had to shelter myself behind its slender trunk as well as I could. One huge bull came straight at me, and shivered one of his horns on the tree, at the spot where I had been standing a moment before. This infuriated the beast to a terrible degree, and he roared and bellowed with pain. I could see that my position would not be

tenable for many moments, and that my only chance
of escape was to get astride one of the savage
brutes. My gymnastic exercises served me in the
time of need. With a bound, I jumped astride of
the nearest, which happened to be an immense cow.
Her astonishment was excessive. She plunged and
danced about, and her hair stood on end with terror.
I held on with the firmness of despair; and how I
managed to keep my seat was a marvel to myself,
and is so still. The other cattle stood in amazement.
My position seemed beyond their comprehension;
but, if it was novel to them, it was equally so to me.
After the cow had exhausted every effort to unseat
me, and was fairly mad with terror, she set off at a
fearful pace over the plain, and made straight for a
small forest of oaks, at which my steed arrived
thoroughly exhausted and subdued, shaking in every
limb. Now was my time—I slipped off, and was up
a tree in an instant.

The danger and excitement had borne me up
until now. I felt faint and giddy; my brow was
hot, my mouth was parched, and my hands were
burning. My first impulse was to offer up a prayer
of gratitude for my preservation and safety. I then
felt my limbs, and found that I had been more
frightened than hurt. I had now recovered my-

self somewhat, and looked around for my as-
sailants.

The cow I had ridden was slowly staggering
towards the herd, which was about a mile off, in
the same position in which I had left them. No
doubt they had watched our course over the plain,
and, perhaps, enjoyed the spectacle as much as more
intelligent animals delight in little less dangerous
sport. To a non-performer our antics must have
been ludicrous beyond compare : the intense terror
of the beast, its efforts to rid itself of its unwelcome
rider, and its career over the plain, must have
afforded great amusement to the bovine spectators ;
as would also the fear depicted on my countenance.
My streaming hair, my knees firmly fixed, and the
clutch I had of the cow's neck, would, altogether,
form a strange picture.

I now descended the tree a little more leisurely
than I ascended it, and walked cautiously along
from tree to tree, with the timid air of a man who
fears the bailiffs. In a short time I got to the open
plain, and took a survey on all sides. I congratulated myself that there was not a bullock to be seen.
The Geelong road was only about a mile off, and
toward it I hurried, as I did not feel altogether
safe after what had occurred. I passed the road,

and struck across the plain in a north-westerly direction. My pace was now quickened, as the sun was near setting, and I had still some miles to go. I did not think much about the beauty of the scenery, or the brilliancy of the sunset, or of the golden and purple clouds that hovered around the sun as he went to rest. I wished that I had the pair of seven-league boots that Jack had, so that I might make one step of it, and get safely housed for the night. My shadow on the ground was becoming longer and longer. As the sun went down, it seemed to go quicker and quicker, until it sank behind the hills. Every moment a darker shade enveloped earth and sky ; every moment another star began to twinkle; every moment another landmark was hidden in the gloom; and every moment I became more conscious that I did not know whither I was going. I was now in a dilemma. I did not like ' bushing it,' although I had often heard of it being done without ill consequences.

However, I determined to make another effort, and tried to guide myself by the stars. Taking Venus for my pilot I walked for about an hour, when, to my joy, I saw a light in the distance, and went towards it as fast as I could. As I got nearer I could see that it was a small fire, and that two men were sitting by it. When I went forward, the men sprang to the opposite side of the fire. I could hear their pistols click as they demanded, ' Who's there ? ' I replied that I had lost my way, and desired that they would allow me to sit by their fire till morning. 'A sneaking spy, by George ! ' said one of them, with a heavy oath. ' Arms above your head, or I 'll put a ball into you. Out with your money ! ' and he pointed his pistol within a few feet of my breast. The other man now came up, tied me to a tree, and then proceeded to rifle my pockets. He found about fifteen pounds in notes, and some loose silver ; also, a small case, containing some papers, of no consequence to any one, and a few of my visiting cards.

When his search was completed, he sat down beside his companion, and examined the papers one by one. He then pulled out my cards and handed one to the tall man, or ' Scotty,' as he called him, and said, ' My card, sir.' Scotty took it and examined it carefully. They now began to talk to each other in whispers. I thought their conversation was about me, for now and again Scotty turned his thumb over his shoulder, toward where I was sitting. I could hear them say, ' Four hundred—Ballarat —Reward—Government—Stockade,' &c. After a long talk of this kind, Scotty again took up the card and looked at it.

'Is that your name?' said he gruffly, looking up at me suddenly.

'Yes,' said I, as gruffly and as suddenly.

'Do you know anything about the Stockade at Ballarat?' said the short man.

I had a key to their conversation in an instant, to the examination of my card, and to the questions they had asked me. I saw that they suspected me to be one of the Ballarat rebels, who was implicated in the disturbances which had taken place a short time before, and for whom, dead or alive, Government was offering a large reward. They thought me to be the man because of the similarity of name, and because I somewhat resembled the so-called rebel. I had now the cards in my own hands, and I determined to play them off to the best advantage, as I expected that they would take me to town and claim the offered reward. I tried to confirm their suspicions as much as possible. I did not answer the question about Ballarat, as I wished to gain time for a reply.

'I think I've see'd you spouting on Bakery Hill,' said the little man. 'You did it up flash too. The mob's uncommon tyrannical, treatin' the diggers like beasts, and neither law nor justice to be had, eh! I remember it all,' said the little man. 'No more license fee, and Maggy Carter and the Bill of Rights,' and the little man roared and laughed until the tears trickled down his cheeks.

'I have seen you drilling under Colonel Vern at the Stockade, have I not?' said I to Scotty.

'No, and —— ' said he, ' when I poo the trigger it's for the hard cash, an' no for ony o' yer nonsensical political balderdash.'

Scotty now jumped to his feet, and said, ' Come, freend, we hae a lang road before us, and ye'll hae a gude horse to ride on, and gude company to guide ye, and ye may consider yoursel as safe as twa ropes can mak ye ; so ye need na be feer't, my man, for ye'll be in Melbourne before mornin', and snugly placed in Wintle's Bank, as a deposit worth four hundred pounds.'

I now solemnly protested that I was not the person they believed me to be ; but they only laughed at me, and told me to ' tell that to the marines,' which I would have been only too glad to do, if any of them had come past our way.

They now brought forward two horses, on one of which they set me. My legs were tied to the saddle, and my arms were still fastened behind my

back. Scotty jumped on the other horse, and
'Slikes,'—for that was the little man's name—got
up behind him. Scotty took the reins of the horse
I was on, and we were soon in motion. I now
feigned to be in despair, and I appealed to their
better feelings if it were right to deliver me up to
certain death for the sake of a few paltry pounds.

'Paltry pounds, d'ye call 'em?' said Slikes;
'why, I'd put a ball through your brain, man, for
ten pounds.'

I wildly offered them all sorts of rewards,
bills of exchange, Government debentures, foreign
securities, Three per Cent. Consols, Spanish bonds,
and railway shares, if they would only take me to
my house in town before daylight, and thus screen
me from the myrmidons of the law who were thirst-
ing for my blood. At every new proposal the two
laughed loud and long, and 'wished I might get it.'

'Well, then,' said I, 'take me to death, take me
to the gallows, let my body swing in ignominy, and
be scoffed and jeered by the unfeeling crowd. I
have done my duty to my country, and my name
shall not be forgotten by her.' Nothing could
exceed their merriment at this burst of assumed
feeling; indeed, during our ride, it was a continual
fund of amusement to them. Whenever their mirth

Q

slacked, Slikes poked me in the ribs with his stick, and shouted, 'No license fee, eh! and Maggy Carter and the Bill of Rights!' When he poked his fun at me in this manner I had a great deal to do to restrain myself from laughing outright. We crossed the Saltwater River just as morning was breaking, and before six o'clock we were at the Police Office, Swanston Street. I was lifted from the saddle and carried in, for my legs were quite benumbed. Scotty walked up to the inspector, and said, 'This is ——, the Ballarat rebel; I give him into your custody, and me and my mate here claim the reward offered for him.' There were two policemen at the door. I shouted 'Policemen, guard the door!' I then turned to the inspector, told him the whole story, and explained who I was. I next gave the men in charge for robbing me. This they denied point-blank. I asked that they might be searched, and I described minutely the notes they had taken from me. When the notes were examined, and found to be as I had described them, Scotty and Slikes became quite confused, and could not say a word for themselves. Their trial came on soon after, and they confessed their guilt. As it was their first offence, they were only sentenced to two years on the roads, with hard labour.

I need hardly say that I was able readily to make myself known to the authorities, and so escape the horrors of martyrdom, or otherwise, that were thought to have been in store for me.

PRINTED BY
SPOTTISWOODE AND CO., NEW-STREET SQUARE
LONDON

POPULAR NOVELS.

By JAMES PAYN.

The Luck of the Darrells.
Thicker than Water.
1s. each, boards; 1s. 6d. each, cloth.

By ANTHONY TROLLOPE.

The Warden.
Barchester Towers.
1s. each, boards; 1s. 6d. each, cloth.

By BRET HARTE.

In the Carquinez Woods.
1s. boards 1s. 6d. cloth.

On the Frontier. 1s.
By Shore and Sedge. 1s.

By ROBERT L. STEVENSON.

The Dynamiter. 1s. sewed; 1s. 6d. cloth.

Strange Case of Dr. Jekyll and Mr. Hyde. 1s. sewed; 1s. 6d. cloth.

By R. L. STEVENSON and L. OSBOURNE.

The Wrong Box. 5s.

By EDNA LYALL.

Autobiography of a Slander. 1s.

By F. ANSTEY.

The Black Poodle, and other Stories. 2s. boards; 2s. 6d. cloth.

By Mrs. DELAND.

John Ward, Preacher. 2s. boards; 2s. 6d. cl th.
Sidney. 6s.

By the Author of the 'ATELIER DU LYS.'

The Atelier du Lys. 2s. 6d.
Mademoiselle Mori. 2s. 6d.
That Child. 2s. 6d.
Under a Cloud. 2s. 6d.
The Fiddler of Lugau. 2s. 6d.
A Child of the Revolution. 2s. 6d.
Hester's Venture. 2s. 6d.
In the Olden Time. 2s. 6d.

By BRANDER MATTHEWS.

A Family Tree; and other Stories. 6s.

By CHRISTIE MURRAY and HY. HERMAN.

Wild Darrie. 2s. boards; 2s. 6d. c oth.

By CHRISTIE MURRAY and HY. MURRAY.

A Dangerous Catspaw. 2s. 6d.

By J. A. FROUDE.

The Two Chiefs of Dunboy. 3s. 6d.

By Mrs. HUGH BELL.

Will o' the Wisp. 3s. 6d.

By WILLIAM O'BRIEN, M.P.

When we were Boys. 2s. 6d.

By the Author of ' THOTH.'

Toxar. 6s.

By JAMES BAKER.

By the Western Sea. 3s. 6d.

By W. E. NORRIS.

Mrs. Fenton : a Sketch. 6s.

London : LONGMANS, GREEN, & CO.

POPULAR NOVELS.

A CATALOGUE OF WORKS

IN

GENERAL LITERATURE

PUBLISHED BY

MESSRS. LONGMANS, GREEN, & CO.,

89 PATERNOSTER ROW, LONDON, E.C.

MESSRS. LONGMANS, GREEN, & CO.

Issue the undermentioned Lists of their Publications, which may be had post free on application :—

1. MONTHLY LIST OF NEW WORKS AND NEW EDITIONS.
2. QUARTERLY LIST OF ANNOUNCE-MENTS AND NEW WORKS.
3. NOTES ON BOOKS; BEING AN ANALYSIS OF THE WORKS PUBLISHED DURING EACH QUARTER.
4. CATALOGUE OF SCIENTIFIC WORKS.
5. CATALOGUE OF MEDICAL AND SURGICAL WORKS.
6. CATALOGUE OF SCHOOL BOOKS AND EDUCATIONAL WORKS.
7. CATALOGUE OF BOOKS FOR ELE-MENTARY SCHOOLS AND PUPIL TEACHERS.
8. CATALOGUE OF THEOLOGICAL WORKS BY DIVINES AND MEMBERS OF THE CHURCH OF ENGLAND.
9. CATALOGUE OF WORKS IN GENERAL LITERATURE.

ABBEY (Rev. C. J.) and OVERTON (Rev. J. H.).—THE ENGLISH CHURCH IN THE EIGHTEENTH CENTURY. Cr. 8vo. 7s. 6d.

ABBOTT (Evelyn).—A HISTORY OF GREECE. In Two Parts.
Part I.—From the Earliest Times to the Ionian Revolt. Cr. 8vo. 10s. 6d.
Part II. Vol. I.—500-445 B.C. [*In the Press.*] Vol. II.—[*In Preparation.*]

—————— HELLENICA. A Collection of Essays on Greek Poetry, Philosophy, History, and Religion. Edited by EVELYN ABBOTT. 8vo. 16s.

ACLAND (A. H. Dyke) and RANSOME (Cyril).—A HANDBOOK IN OUTLINE OF THE POLITICAL HISTORY OF ENGLAND TO 1890. Chronologically Arranged. Crown 8vo. 6s.

ACTON (Eliza).—MODERN COOKERY. With 150 Woodcuts. Fcp. 8vo. 4s. 6d.

A. K. H. B.—THE ESSAYS AND CONTRIBUTIONS OF.   Crown 8v
3s. 6d. each.

Autumn Holidays of a Country Parson.
Changed Aspects of Unchanged
    Truths.
Commonplace Philosopher.
Counsel and Comfort from a City
    Pulpit.
Critical Essays of a Country Parson.
East Coast Days and Memories.
Graver Thoughts of a Country Parson.
    Three Series.
Landscapes, Churches, and Moralities.

Leisure Hours in Town.
Lessons of Middle Age.
Our Little Life.   Two Series.
Our Homely Comedy and Tragedy.
Present Day Thoughts.
Recreations of a Country Parson.
    Three Series.
Seaside Musings.
Sunday Afternoons in the Pari
    Church of a Scottish Universi
    City.

———— 'To Meet the Day' through the Christian Year; being a Text of Scri
ture, with an Original Meditation and a Short Selection in Verse for Eve
Day.   Crown 8vo. 4s. 6d.

AMERICAN WHIST, Illustrated : containing the Laws and Principles of tl
Game, the Analysis of the New Play.   By G. W. P.   Fcp. 8vo. 6s. 6d.

AMOS (Sheldon).—A PRIMER OF THE ENGLISH CONSTITUTIO
AND GOVERNMENT.   Crown 8vo. 6s.

ANNUAL REGISTER (The).   A Review of Public Events at Home and Abroa
for the year 1890.   8vo. 18s.
*** Volumes of the 'Annual Register' for the years 1863-1889 can still be ha

ANSTEY (F.).—THE BLACK POODLE, and other Stories.   Crown 8v
2s. boards. ; 2s. 6d. cloth.

———— VOCES POPULI.   Reprinted from *Punch*.   First Series, with 20 Illu
trations by J. BERNARD PARTRIDGE.   Fcp. 4to. 5s.

ARISTOTLE—The Works of.
———— THE POLITICS, G. Bekker's Greek Text of Books I. III. IV. (VII
with an English Translation by W. E. BOLLAND, and short Introducto
Essays by ANDREW LANG.   Crown 8vo. 7s. 6d.

———— THE POLITICS, Introductory Essays.   By ANDREW LANG.   (Frc
Bolland and Lang's ' Politics '.)   Crown 8vo. 2s. 6d.

———— THE ETHICS, Greek Text, illustrated with Essays and Notes.   By S
ALEXANDER GRANT, Bart.   2 vols. 8vo. 32s.

———— THE NICOMACHEAN ETHICS, newly translated into English.   ]
ROBERT WILLIAMS.   Crown 8vo. 7s. 6d.

ARMSTRONG (Ed.).—ELISABETH FARNESE : the Termagant
Spain.

ARMSTRONG (G. F. Savage-).—POEMS : Lyrical and Dramatic.   Fc
8vo. 6s.
BY THE SAME AUTHOR.   Fcp. 8vo.

King Saul.   5s.
King David.   5s.
King Solomon.   6s.
Ugone ; a Tragedy.   6s.
A Garland from Greece.   Poems.   9s.

. Stories of Wicklow.   Poems.   9s.
Mephistopheles in Broadcloth ; a S
    tire.   4s.
The Life and Letters of Edmond
    Armstrong.   7s. 6d.

ARMSTRONG (E. J.).—POETICAL WORKS.   Fcp. 8vo. 5s.
———— ESSAYS AND SKETCHES.   Fcp. 8vo. 5s.

ARNOLD (Sir Edwin).—THE LIGHT OF THE WORLD, or the Great Consummation. A Poem. Crown 8vo. *7s. 6d. net.*

———— SEAS AND LANDS. Reprinted by the permission of the proprietors of the *Daily Telegraph*, from Letters published under the title 'By Sea and Land' in that Journal. Illustrated. 8vo. *21s.*

ARNOLD (Dr. T.).—INTRODUCTORY LECTURES ON MODERN HISTORY. 8vo. *7s. 6d.*

———— MISCELLANEOUS WORKS. 8vo. *7s. 6d.*

ASHLEY (J. W.).—ENGLISH ECONOMIC HISTORY AND THEORY. Part I.—The Middle Ages. Crown 8vo. *5s.*

ATELIER (The) du Lys; or, An Art Student in the Reign of Terror. By the Author of 'Mademoiselle Mori'. Crown 8vo. *2s. 6d.*

BY THE SAME AUTHOR. Crown 2s. 6d. each.

MADEMOISELLE MORI. .	A CHILD OF THE REVOLU-
THAT CHILD.	TION.
UNDER A CLOUD.	HESTER'S VENTURE.
THE FIDDLER OF LUGAU.	IN THE OLDEN TIME.

BACON.—COMPLETE WORKS. Edited by R. L. ELLIS, J. SPEDDING, and D. D. HEATH. 7 vols. 8vo. £3 *13s. 6d.*

———— LETTERS AND LIFE, INCLUDING ALL HIS OCCASIONAL WORKS. Edited by J. SPEDDING. 7 vols. 8vo. £4 *4s.*

———— THE ESSAYS; with Annotations. By Archbishop WHATELY. 8vo. *10s. 6d.*

———— THE ESSAYS; with Introduction, Notes, and Index. By E. A. ABBOTT. 2 vols. Fcp. 8vo. *6s.* Text and Index only. Fcp. 8vo. *2s. 6d.*

BADMINTON LIBRARY (The), edited by the DUKE OF BEAUFORT, assisted by ALFRED E. T. WATSON.

HUNTING. By the DUKE OF BEAUFORT, and MOWBRAY MORRIS. With 53 Illustrations. Crown 8vo. *10s. 6d.*

FISHING. By H. CHOLMONDELEY-PENNELL.
  Vol. I. Salmon, Trout, and Grayling. 158 Illustrations. Crown 8vo. *10s. 6d.*
  Vol. II. Pike and other Coarse Fish. 132 Illustrations. Crown 8vo. *10s. 6d.*

RACING AND STEEPLECHASING. By the EARL OF SUFFOLK AND BERKSHIRE, W. G. CRAVEN, &c. 56 Illustrations. Crown 8vo. *10s. 6d.*

SHOOTING. By LORD WALSINGHAM, and Sir RALPH PAYNE-GALLWEY, Bart.
  Vol. I. Field and Covert. With 105 Illustrations. Crown 8vo. *10s. 6d.*
  Vol. II. Moor and Marsh. With 65 Illustrations. Crown 8vo. *10s. 6d.*

CYCLING. By VISCOUNT BURY (Earl of Albemarle) and G. LACY HILLIER. With 89 Illustrations. Crown 8vo. *10s. 6d.*

ATHLETICS AND FOOTBALL. By MONTAGUE SHEARMAN. With 41 Illustrations. Crown 8vo. *10s. 6d.*

BOATING. By W. B. WOODGATE. With 49 Illustrations. Crown 8vo. *10s. 6d.*

CRICKET. By A. G. STEEL and the Hon. R. H. LYTTELTON. With 63 Illustrations. Crown 8vo. *10s. 6d.*

DRIVING. By the DUKE OF BEAUFORT. With 65 Illustrations. Crown 8vo. *10s. 6d.*

[Continued.

BADMINTON LIBRARY (The)—*(continued)*.

FENCING, BOXING, AND WRESTLING. By WALTER H. POLLOCK, F. C. GROVE, C. PREVOST, E. B. MICHELL, and WALTER ARMSTRONG. With 42 Illustrations. Crown 8vo. 10s. 6d.

GOLF. By HORACE HUTCHINSON, the Rt. Hon. A. J. BALFOUR, M.P., ANDREW LANG, Sir W. G. SIMPSON, Bart., &c. With 88 Illustrations. Crown 8vo. 10s. 6d.

TENNIS, LAWN TENNIS, RACKETS, AND FIVES. By J. M. and C. G. HEATHCOTE, E. O. PLEYDELL-BOUVERIE, and A. C. AINGER. With 79 Illustrations. Crown 8vo. 10s. 6d.

RIDING AND POLO. By Captain ROBERT WEIR, Riding-Master, R.H.G., J. MORAY BROWN, &c. With 59 Illustrations. Crown 8vo. 10s. 6d.

BAGEHOT (Walter).—BIOGRAPHICAL STUDIES. 8vo. 12s.

—————— ECONOMIC STUDIES. 8vo. 10s. 6d.

—————— LITERARY STUDIES. 2 vols. 8vo. 28s.

—————— THE POSTULATES OF ENGLISH POLITICAL ECONOMY. Crown 8vo. 2s. 6d.

—————— A PRACTICAL PLAN FOR ASSIMILATING THE ENGLISH AND AMERICAN MONEY AS A STEP TOWARDS A UNIVERSAL MONEY. Crown 8vo. 2s. 6d.

BAGWELL (Richard).—IRELAND UNDER THE TUDORS. (3 vols.) Vols. I. and II. From the first invasion of the Northmen to the year 1578. 8vo. 32s. Vol. III. 1578-1603. 8vo. 18s.

BAIN (Alex.).—MENTAL AND MORAL SCIENCE. Crown 8vo. 10s. 6d.

—————— SENSES AND THE INTELLECT. 8vo. 15s.

—————— EMOTIONS AND THE WILL. 8vo. 15s.

—————— LOGIC, DEDUCTIVE AND INDUCTIVE. Part I., *Deduction*, 4s. Part II., *Induction*, 6s. 6d.

—————— PRACTICAL ESSAYS. Crown 8vo. 2s.

BAKER (James).—BY THE WESTERN SEA: a Novel. Cr. 8vo. 3s. 6d.

BAKER.—EIGHT YEARS IN CEYLON. With 6 Illustrations. Crown 8vo. 3s. 6d.

—————— THE RIFLE AND THE HOUND IN CEYLON. With 6 Illustrations. Crown 8vo. 3s. 6d.

BALL (The Rt. Hon. T. J.).—THE REFORMED CHURCH OF IRELAND (1537-1889). 8vo. 7s. 6d.

—————— HISTORICAL REVIEW OF THE LEGISLATIVE SYSTEMS OPERATIVE IN IRELAND (1172-1800). 8vo. 6s.

BEACONSFIELD (The Earl of).—NOVELS AND TALES. The Hughenden Edition. With 2 Portraits and 11 Vignettes. 11 vols. Crown 8vo. 42s.

Endymion.	Venetia.	Alroy, Ixion, &c.
Lothair.	Henrietta Temple.	The Young Duke,. &c.
Coningsby.	Contarini Fleming, &c.	Vivian Grey.
Tancred. Sybil.		

NOVELS AND TALES. Cheap Edition. 11 vols. Crown 8vo. 1s. each, boards; 1s. 6d. each, cloth.

BECKER (Professor).—GALLUS; or, Roman Scenes in the Time of Augustus. Post 8vo. 7s. 6d.

———— CHARICLES; or, Illustrations of the Private Life of the Ancient Greeks Post 8vo. 7s. 6d.

BELL (Mrs. Hugh).—WILL O' THE WISP: a Story. Crown 8vo. 3s. 6d.

———— CHAMBER COMEDIES. Crown 8vo. 6s.

BLAKE (J.).—TABLES FOR THE CONVERSION OF 5 PER CENT. IN-TEREST FROM ⅛ TO 7 PER CENT. 8vo. 12s. 6d.

BOOK (THE) OF WEDDING DAYS. Arranged on the Plan of a Birthday Book. With 96 Illustrated Borders, Frontispiece, and Title-page by Walter Crane; and Quotations for each Day. Compiled and Arranged by K. E. J. REID, MAY ROSS, and MABEL BAMFIELD. 4to. 21s.

BRASSEY (Lady).—A VOYAGE IN THE 'SUNBEAM,' OUR HOME ON THE OCEAN FOR ELEVEN MONTHS.
Library Edition. With 8 Maps and Charts, and 118 Illustrations, 8vo. 21s.
Cabinet Edition. With Map and 66 Illustrations, Crown 8vo. 7s. 6d.
Cheap Edition. With 66 Illustrations, Crown 8vo. 3s. 6d.
School Edition. With 37 Illustrations, Fcp. 2s. cloth, or 3s. white parchment.
Popular Edition. With 60 Illustrations, 4to. 6d. sewed, 1s. cloth.

———— SUNSHINE AND STORM IN THE EAST.
Library Edition. With 2 Maps and 114 Illustrations, 8vo. 21s.
Cabinet Edition. With 2 Maps and 114 Illustrations, Crown 8vo. 7s. 6d.
Popular Edition. With 103 Illustrations, 4to. 6d. sewed, 1s. cloth.

———— IN THE TRADES, THE TROPICS, AND THE 'ROARING FORTIES'.
Cabinet Edition. With Map and 220 Illustrations, Crown 8vo. 7s. 6d.
Popular Edition. With 183 Illustrations, 4to. 6d. sewed, 1s. cloth.

———— THE LAST VOYAGE TO INDIA AND AUSTRALIA IN THE 'SUNBEAM'. With Charts and Maps, and 40 Illustrations in Monotone (20 full-page), and nearly 200 Illustrations in the Text. 8vo. 21s.

———— THREE VOYAGES IN THE 'SUNBEAM'. Popular Edition. With 346 Illustrations, 4to. 2s. 6d.

BRAY (Charles).—THE PHILOSOPHY OF NECESSITY; or, Law in Mind as in Matter. Crown 8vo. 5s.

BRIGHT (Rev. J. Franck).—A HISTORY OF ENGLAND. 4 vols. Cr. 8vo.
Period I.—Mediæval Monarchy: The Departure of the Romans to Richard III. From A.D. 449 to 1485. 4s. 6d.
Period II.—Personal Monarchy: Henry VII. to James II. From 1485 to 1688. 5s.
Period III.—Constitutional Monarchy: William and Mary to William IV. From 1689 to 1837. 7s. 6d.
Period IV.—The Growth of Democracy: Victoria. From 1837 to 1880. 6s.

BRYDEN (H. A.).—KLOOF AND KARROO: Sport, Legend, and Natural History in Cape Colony. With 17 Illustrations. 8vo. 10s. 6d.

BUCKLE (Henry Thomas).—HISTORY OF CIVILISATION IN ENG-LAND AND FRANCE, SPAIN AND SCOTLAND. 3 vols. Cr. 8vo. 24s.

BULL (Thomas).—HINTS TO MOTHERS ON THE MANAGEMENT OF THEIR HEALTH during the Period of Pregnancy. Fcp. 8vo. 1s. 6d.
———— THE MATERNAL MANAGEMENT OF CHILDREN IN HEALTH AND DISEASE. Fcp. 8vo. 1s. 6d.

BUTLER (Samuel).—EREWHON. Crown 8vo. 5s.
———— THE FAIR HAVEN. A Work in Defence of the Miraculous Element in our Lord's Ministry. Crown 8vo. 7s. 6d.
———— LIFE AND HABIT. An Essay after a Completer View of Evolution. Cr. 8vo. 7s. 6d.
———— EVOLUTION, OLD AND NEW. Crown 8vo. 10s. 6d.
———— UNCONSCIOUS MEMORY. Crown 8vo. 7s. 6d.
———— ALPS AND SANCTUARIES OF PIEDMONT AND THE CANTON TICINO. Illustrated. Pott 4to. 10s. 6d.
———— SELECTIONS FROM WORKS. Crown 8vo. 7s. 6d.
———— LUCK, OR CUNNING, AS THE MAIN MEANS OF ORGANIC MODIFICATION? Crown 8vo. 7s. 6d.
———— EX VOTO. An Account of the Sacro Monte or New Jerusalem at Varallo-Sesia. Crown 8vo. 10s. 6d.
———— HOLBEIN'S 'LA DANSE'. 3s.

CARLYLE (Thomas).—THOMAS CARLYLE: a History of his Life. By J. A. FROUDE. 1795-1835, 2 vols. Cr. 8vo. 7s. 1834-1881, 2 vols. Cr. 8vo. 7s.

CASE (Thomas).—PHYSICAL REALISM : being an Analytical Philosophy from the Physical Objects of Science to the Physical Data of Sense. 8vo. 15s.

CHETWYND (Sir George).—RACING REMINISCENCES AND EXPERIENCES OF THE TURF. 2 vols. 8vo. 21s.

CHILD (Gilbert W.).—CHURCH AND STATE UNDER THE TUDORS. 8vo. 15s.

CHISHOLM (G. G.).—HANDBOOK OF COMMERCIAL GEOGRAPHY. With 29 Maps. 8vo. 16s.

CHURCH (Sir Richard).—Commander-in-Chief of the Greeks in the War of Independence: a Memoir. By STANLEY LANE-POOLE. 8vo. 5s.

CLIVE (Mrs. Archer).—POEMS. Including the IX. Poems. Fcp. 8vo. 6s.

CLODD (Edward).—THE STORY OF CREATION : a Plain Account of Evolution. With 77 Illustrations. Crown 8vo. 3s. 6d.

CLUTTERBUCK (W. J.).—THE SKIPPER IN ARCTIC SEAS. With 39 Illustrations. Crown 8vo. 10s. 6d.
———— ABOUT CEYLON AND BORNEO : being an Account of Two Visits to Ceylon, one to Borneo, and How we Fell Out on our Homeward Journey. With 47 Illustrations. Crown 8vo.

COLENSO (J. W.).—THE PENTATEUCH AND BOOK OF JOSHUA CRITICALLY EXAMINED. Crown 8vo. 6s.

COMYN (L. N.).—ATHERSTONE PRIORY: a Tale. Crown 8vo. 2s. 6d.

CONINGTON (John).—THE ÆNEID OF VIRGIL. Translated into English Verse. Crown 8vo. 6s.
———— THE POEMS OF VIRGIL. Translated into English Prose. Cr. 8vo. 6s.

COX (Rev. Sir G. W.).—A HISTORY OF GREECE, from the Earliest Period to the Death of Alexander the Great. With 11 Maps. Cr. 8vo. 7s. 6d.

CRAKE (Rev. A. D.).—HISTORICAL TALES. Cr. 8vo. 5 vols. 2s. 6d. each.

Edwy the Fair; or, The First Chronicle of Æscendune.

Alfgar the Dane; or, The Second Chronicle of Æscendune.

The Rival Heirs : being the Third and Last Chronicle of Æscendune.

The House of Walderne. A Tale of the Cloister and the Forest in the Days of the Barons' Wars.

Brian Fitz-Count. A Story of Wallingford Castle and Dorchester Abbey.

——— HISTORY OF THE CHURCH UNDER THE ROMAN EMPIRE, A.D. 30-476. Crown 8vo. 7s. 6d.

CREIGHTON (Mandell, D.D.).—HISTORY OF THE PAPACY DURING THE REFORMATION. 8vo. Vols. I. and II., 1378-1464, 32s. ; Vols. III. and IV., 1464-1518, 24s.

CRUMP (A.).—A SHORT ENQUIRY INTO THE FORMATION OF POLITICAL OPINION, from the Reign of the Great Families to the Advent, of Democracy. 8vo. 7s. 6d.

——— AN INVESTIGATION INTO THE CAUSES OF THE GREAT FALL IN PRICES which took place coincidently with the Demonetisation of Silver by Germany. 8vo. 6s.

CURZON (Hon. George N.).—RUSSIA IN CENTRAL ASIA IN 1889 AND THE ANGLO-RUSSIAN QUESTION. 8vo. 21s.

DANTE.—LA COMMEDIA DI DANTE. A New Text, carefully Revised with the aid of the most recent Editions and Collations. Small 8vo. 6s.

DE LA SAUSSAYE (Prof. Chantepie).—A MANUAL OF THE SCIENCE OF RELIGION. Translated by Mrs. COLYER FERGUSSON (née MAX MÜLLER). Crown 8vo. 12s. 6d.

DELAND (Mrs.).—JOHN WARD, PREACHER. Cr. 8vo. 2s. bds., 2s. 6d. cl.

——— SIDNEY : a Novel. Crown 8vo. 6s.

——— THE OLD GARDEN, and other Verses. Fcp. 8vo. 5s.

DE REDCLIFFE.—THE LIFE OF THE RIGHT HON. STRATFORD CANNING : VISCOUNT STRATFORD DE REDCLIFFE. By STANLEY LANE-POOLE. With 3 Portraits. Crown 8vo. 7s. 6d.

DE SALIS (Mrs.).—Works by :—

Cakes and Confections à la Mode. Fcp. 8vo. 1s. 6d.

Dressed Game and Poultry à la Mode. Fcp. 8vo. 1s. 6d.

Dressed Vegetables à la Mode. Fcp. 8vo. 1s. 6d.

Drinks à la Mode. Fcp. 8vo. 1s. 6d.

Entrées à la Mode. Fcp. 1s. 8vo. 6d.

Floral Decorations. Fcp. 8vo. 1s. 6d.

Oysters à la Mode. Fcp. 8vo. 1s. 6d.

Puddings and Pastry à la Mode. Fcp. 8vo. 1s. 6d.

Savouries à la Mode. Fcp. 8vo. 1s. 6d.

Soups and Dressed Fish à la Mode. Fcp. 8vo. 1s. 6d.

Sweets and Supper Dishes à la Mode. Fcp. 8vo. 1s. 6d.

Tempting Dishes for Small Incomes. Fcp. 8vo. 1s. 6d.

Wrinkles and Notions for every Household. Crown 8vo. 2s. 6d.

DE TOCQUEVILLE (Alexis).—DEMOCRACY IN AMERICA. Translated by HENRY REEVE, C.B. 2 vols. Crown 8vo. 16s.

DOWELL (Stephen).—A HISTORY OF TAXATION AND TAXES IN ENGLAND. 4 vols. 8vo. Vols. I and II., The History of Taxation, 21s. Vols. III. and IV., The History of Taxes, 21s.

DOYLE (A. Conan).—MICAH CLARKE : a Tale of Monmouth's Rebellion. With Frontispiece and Vignette. Crown 8vo. 3s. 6d.

——— THE CAPTAIN OF THE POLESTAR ; and other Tales. Cr. 8vo. 6s.

DRANE (Augusta T.).—THE HISTORY OF ST. DOMINIC, FOUNDER OF THE FRIAR PREACHERS. With 32 Illustrations. 8vo. 15s.

DUBLIN UNIVERSITY PRESS SERIES (The): a Series of Works undertaken by the Provost and Senior Fellows of Trinity College, Dublin.

Abbott's (T. K.) Codex Rescriptus Dublinensis of St. Matthew. 4to. 21s.
—— Evangeliorum Versio Antehieronymiana ex Codice Usseriano (Dublinensi). 2 vols. Cr. 8vo. 21s.
Allman's (G. J.) Greek Geometry from Thales to Euclid. 8vo. 10s. 6d.
Burnside (W. S.) and Panton's (A. W.) Theory of Equations. 8vo. 12s. 6d.
Casey's (John) Sequel to Euclid's Elements. Crown 8vo. 3s. 6d.
—— Analytical Geometry of the Conic Sections. Crown 8vo. 7s. 6d.
Davies' (J. F.) Eumenides of Æschylus, With Metrical English Translation. 8vo. 7s.
Dublin Translations into Greek and Latin Verse. Edited by R. Y. Tyrrell. 8vo. 6s.
Graves' (R. P.) Life of Sir William Hamilton. 3 vols. 15s. each.
Griffin (R. W.) on Parabola, Ellipse, and Hyperbola. Crown 8vo. 6s.
Hobart's (W. K.) Medical Language of St. Luke. 8vo. 16s.
Leslie's (T. E. Cliffe) Essays in Political Economy. 8vo. 10s. 6d.
Macalister's (A.) Zoology and Morphology of Vertebrata. 8vo. 10s. 6d.
MacCullagh's (James) Mathematical and other Tracts. 8vo. 15s.

Maguire's (T.) Parmenides of Plato, Text with Introduction, Analysis, &c. 8vo. 7s. 6d.
Monck's (W. H. S.) Introduction to Logic. Crown 8vo. 5s.
Roberts' (R. A.) Examples on the Analytic Geometry of Plane Conics. Crown 8vo. 5s.
Southey's (R.) Correspondence with Caroline Bowles. Edited by E. Dowden. 8vo. 14s.
Stubbs' (J. W.) History of the University of Dublin, from its Foundation to the End of the Eighteenth Century. 8vo. 12s. 6d.
Thornhill's (W. J.) The Æneid of Virgil, freely translated into English Blank Verse. Crown 8vo. 7s. 6d.
Tyrrell's (R. Y.) Cicero's Correspondence.
Vols. I., II. and III. 8vo. each 12s.
—— The Acharnians of Aristophanes, translated into English Verse. Crown 8vo. 1s.
Webb's (T. E.) Goethe's Faust, Translation and Notes. 8vo. 12s. 6d.
—— The Veil of Isis; a Series of Essays on Idealism. 8vo. 10s. 6d.
Wilkins' (G.) The Growth of the Homeric Poems. 8vo. 6s.

EWALD (Heinrich).—THE ANTIQUITIES OF ISRAEL. 8vo. 12s. 6d.

—— THE HISTORY OF ISRAEL. 8vo. Vols. I. and II. 24s. Vols. III. and IV. 21s. Vol. V. 18s. Vol. VI. 16s. Vol. VII. 21s. Vol. VIII. 18s.

FARNELL (G. S.).—THE GREEK LYRIC POETS. 8vo. 16s.

FARRAR (F. W.).—LANGUAGE AND LANGUAGES. Crown 8vo. 6s.

—— DARKNESS AND DAWN; or, Scenes in the Days of Nero. An Historic Tale. 2 vols. 8vo. 28s.

FIRTH (J. C.).—NATION MAKING: a Story of New Zealand Savageism and Civilisation. Crown 8vo. 6s.

FITZWYGRAM (Major-General Sir F.).—HORSES AND STABLES. With 19 pages of Illustrations. 8vo. 5s.

FORD (Horace).—THE THEORY AND PRACTICE OF ARCHERY. New Edition, thoroughly Revised and Re-written by W. BUTT. 8vo. 14s.

FOUARD (Abbé Constant).—THE CHRIST THE SON OF GOD. With Introduction by Cardinal Manning. 2 vols. Crown 8vo. 14s.

FOX (C. J.).—THE EARLY HISTORY OF CHARLES JAMES FOX. By the Right Hon. Sir. G. O. TREVELYAN, Bart.
Library Edition. 8vo. 18s. | Cabinet Edition. Crown 8vo. 6s.

FRANCIS (Francis).—A BOOK ON ANGLING : including full Illustrated Lists of Salmon Flies. Post 8vo. 15s.

FREEMAN (E. A.).—THE HISTORICAL GEOGRAPHY OF EUROPE. With 65 Maps. 2 vols. 8vo. 31s. 6d.

FROUDE (James A.).—THE HISTORY OF ENGLAND, from the Fall of Wolsey to the Defeat of the Spanish Armada. 12 vols. Crown 8vo. £2 2s.

———— THE DIVORCE OF CATHERINE OF ARAGON : The Story as told by the Imperial Ambassadors resident at the Court of Henry VIII. *In Usum Laicorum.* 8vo. 16s.

———— THE ENGLISH IN IRELAND IN THE EIGHTEENTH CENTURY. 3 vols. Crown 8vo. 18s.

———— SHORT STUDIES ON GREAT SUBJECTS.
Cabinet Edition. 4 vols. Cr. 8vo. 24s. | Cheap Edit. 4 vols. Cr. 8vo. 3s. 6d. ea.

———— CÆSAR : a Sketch. Crown 8vo. 3s. 6d.

———— OCEANA ; OR, ENGLAND AND HER COLONIES. With 9 Illustrations. Crown 8vo. 2s. boards, 2s. 6d. cloth.

———— THE ENGLISH IN THE WEST INDIES; or, the Bow of Ulysses. With 9 Illustrations. Crown 8vo. 2s. boards, 2s. 6d. cloth.

———— THE TWO CHIEFS OF DUNBOY; an Irish Romance of the Last Century. Crown 8vo. 3s. 6d.

———— THOMAS CARLYLE, a History of his Life. 1795 to 1835. 2 vols. Crown 8vo. 7s. 1834 to 1881. 2 vols. Crown 8vo. 7s.

GALLWEY (Sir Ralph Payne-).—LETTERS TO YOUNG SHOOTERS. (First Series.) On the Choice and Use of a Gun. Crown 8vo. 7s. 6d.

GARDINER (Samuel Rawson).—HISTORY OF ENGLAND, 1603-1642. 10 vols. Crown 8vo. price 6s. each.

———— A HISTORY OF THE GREAT CIVIL WAR, 1642-1649. (3 vols.) Vol. I. 1642-1644. With 24 Maps. 8vo. 21s. *(out of print).* Vol. II. 1644-1647. With 21 Maps. 8vo. 24s. Vol. III. 1647-1649.

———— THE STUDENT'S HISTORY OF ENGLAND. Vol. I. B.C. 55-A.D. 1509, with 173 Illustrations, Crown 8vo. 4s. Vol. II. 1509-1689, with 96 Illustrations. Crown 8vo. 4s. Vol. III. 1689-1885, with Illustrations. Crown 8vo. 4s. Complete in 1 vol. Crown 8vo. 12s.

———— A SCHOOL ATLAS OF ENGLISH HISTORY. A Companion Atlas to ' Student's History of England '. 66 Maps and 22 Plans. Fcap. 4to. 5s.

GIBERNE (Agnes).—NIGEL BROWNING. Crown 8vo. 5s.

GOETHE.—FAUST. A New Translation chiefly in Blank Verse ; with Introduction and Notes. By JAMES ADEY BIRDS. Crown 8vo. 6s.

———— FAUST. The Second Part. A New Translation in Verse. By JAMES ADEY BIRDS. Crown 8vo. 6s.

GREEN (T. H.)—THE WORKS OF THOMAS HILL GREEN. (3 Vols.) Vols. I. and II. 8vo. 16s. each. Vol. III. 8vo. 21s.

———— THE WITNESS OF GOD AND FAITH : Two Lay Sermons. Fcp. 8vo. 2s.

GREVILLE (C. C. F.).—A JOURNAL OF THE REIGNS OF KING GEORGE IV., KING WILLIAM IV., AND QUEEN VICTORIA. Edited by H. REEVE. 8 vols. Crown 8vo. 6s. each.

GWILT (Joseph).—AN ENCYCLOPÆDIA OF ARCHITECTURE. With more than 1700 Engravings on Wood. 8vo. 52*s*. 6*d*.

HAGGARD (Ella).—LIFE AND ITS AUTHOR : an Essay in Verse. With a Memoir by H. Rider Haggard, and Portrait. Fcp. 8vo. 3*s*. 6*d*.

HAGGARD (H. Rider).—SHE. With 32 Illustrations. Crown 8vo. 3*s*. 6*d*.
———— ALLAN QUATERMAIN. With 31 Illustrations. Crown 8vo. 3*s*. 6*d*.
———— MAIWA'S REVENGE. Crown 8vo. 1*s*. boards, 1*s*. 6*d*. cloth.
———— COLONEL QUARITCH, V.C. Crown 8vo. 3*s*. 6*d*.
———— CLEOPATRA : With 29 Illustrations. Crown 8vo. 3*s*. 6*d*.
———— BEATRICE. Crown 8vo. 6*s*.
———— ERIC BRIGHTEYES. With 51 Illustrations. Crown 8vo. 6*s*.

HAGGARD (H. Rider) and LANG (Andrew).—THE WORLD'S DESIRE. Crown 8vo. 6*s*.

HALLIWELL-PHILLIPPS (J. O.)—A CALENDAR OF THE HALLI-WELL-PHILLIPPS COLLECTION OF SHAKESPEAREAN RARITIES. Second Edition. Enlarged by Ernest E. Baker. 8vo. 10*s*. 6*d*.
———— OUTLINE OF THE LIFE OF SHAKESPEARE. 2 vols. Royal 8vo. 21*s*.

HARRISON (Jane E.).—MYTHS OF THE ODYSSEY IN ART AND LITERATURE. Illustrated with Outline Drawings. 8vo. 18*s*.

HARRISON (F. Bayford).—THE CONTEMPORARY HISTORY OF THE FRENCH REVOLUTION. Crown 8vo. 3*s*. 6*d*.

HARTE (Bret).—IN THE CARQUINEZ WOODS. Fcp. 8vo. 1*s*. bds., 1*s*. 6*d*. cloth.
———— BY SHORE AND SEDGE. 16mo. 1*s*.
———— ON THE FRONTIER. 16mo. 1*s*.

HARTWIG (Dr.).—THE SEA AND ITS LIVING WONDERS. With 12 Plates and 303 Woodcuts. 8vo. 10*s*. 6*d*.
THE TROPICAL WORLD. With 8 Plates and 172 Woodcuts. 8vo. 10*s*. 6*d*.
THE POLAR WORLD. With 3 Maps, 8 Plates and 85 Woodcuts. 8vo. 10*s*. 6*d*.
THE SUBTERRANEAN WORLD. With 3 Maps and 80 Woodcuts. 8vo. 10*s*. 6*d*.
THE AERIAL WORLD. With Map, 8 Plates and 60 Woodcuts. 8vo. 10*s*. 6*d*.

HAVELOCK.—MEMOIRS OF SIR HENRY HAVELOCK, K.C.B. By JOHN CLARK MARSHMAN. Crown 8vo. 3*s*. 6*d*.

HEARN (W. Edward).—THE GOVERNMENT OF ENGLAND : its Structure and its Development. 8vo. 16*s*.
———— THE ARYAN HOUSEHOLD : its Structure and ts Development. An Introduction to Comparative Jurisprudence. 8vo. 16*s*.

HISTORIC TOWNS. Edited by E. A. FREEMAN and Rev. WILLIAM HUNT. With Maps and Plans. Crown 8vo. 3*s*. 6*d*. each.

Bristol. By Rev. W. Hunt.
Carlisle. By Dr. Mandell Creighton.
Cinque Ports. By Montagu Burrows.
Colchester. By Rev. E. L. Cutts.
Exeter. By E. A. Freeman.
London. By Rev. W. J. Loftie.
Oxford. By Rev. C. W. Boase.

Winchester. By Rev. G. W. Kitchin.
New York. By Theodore Roosevelt.
Boston (U.S.). By Henry Cabot Lodge.
York. By Rev. James Raine.
[*In preparation.*

HODGSON (Shadworth H.).—TIME AND SPACE: a Metaphysical Essay. 8vo. 16s.

——— THE THEORY OF PRACTICE: an Ethical Enquiry. 2 vols. 8vo. 24s.

——— THE PHILOSOPHY OF REFLECTION. 2 vols. 8vo. 21s.

——— OUTCAST ESSAYS AND VERSE TRANSLATIONS. Crown 8vo. 8s. 6d.

HOWITT (William).—VISITS TO REMARKABLE PLACES. 80 Illustrations. Crown 8vo. 3s. 6d.

HULLAH (John).—COURSE OF LECTURES ON THE HISTORY OF MODERN MUSIC. 8vo. 8s. 6d.

——— COURSE OF LECTURES ON THE TRANSITION PERIOD OF MUSICAL HISTORY. 8vo. 10s. 6d.

HUME.—THE PHILOSOPHICAL WORKS OF DAVID HUME. Edited by T. H. GREEN and T. H. GROSE. 4 vols. 8vo. 56s.

HUTCHINSON (Horace).—CREATURES OF CIRCUMSTANCE: a Novel. 3 vols. Crown 8vo. 25s. 6d.

——— FAMOUS GOLF LINKS. By HORACE G. HUTCHINSON, ANDREW LANG, H. S. C. EVERARD, T. RUTHERFORD CLARK, &c. With numerous Illustrations by F. P. Hopkins, T. Hodges, H. S. King, &c. Crown 8vo. 6s.

HUTH (Alfred H.).—THE MARRIAGE OF NEAR KIN. Royal 8vo. 21s.

INGELOW (Jean).—POETICAL WORKS. Vols. I. and II. Fcp. 8vo. 12s. Vol. III. Fcp. 8vo. 5s.

——— LYRICAL AND OTHER POEMS. Selected from the Writings of JEAN INGELOW. Fcp. 8vo. 2s. 6d. cloth plain, 3s. cloth gilt.

——— VERY YOUNG and QUITE ANOTHER STORY: Two Stories. Crown 8vo. 6s.

JAMESON (Mrs.).—SACRED AND LEGENDARY ART. With 19 Etchings and 187 Woodcuts. 2 vols. 8vo. 20s. net.

——— LEGENDS OF THE MADONNA, the Virgin Mary as represented in Sacred and Legendary Art. With 27 Etchings and 165 Woodcuts. 8vo. 10s. net.

——— LEGENDS OF THE MONASTIC ORDERS. With 11 Etchings and 88 Woodcuts. 8vo. 10s. net.

——— HISTORY OF OUR LORD. His Types and Precursors. Completed by LADY EASTLAKE. With 31 Etchings and 281 Woodcuts. 2 vols. 8vo. 20s. net.

JEFFERIES (Richard).—FIELD AND HEDGEROW. Last Essays. Crown 8vo. 3s. 6d.

——— THE STORY OF MY HEART: My Autobiography. Crown 8vo. 3s. 6d.

JENNINGS (Rev. A. C.).—ECCLESIA ANGLICANA. A History of the Church of Christ in England. Crown 8vo. 7s. 6d.

JESSOP (G. H.).—JUDGE LYNCH: a Tale of the California Vineyards. Crown 8vo. 6s.

JOHNSON (J. & J. H.).—THE PATENTEE'S MANUAL; a Treatise on the Law and Practice of Letters Patent. 8vo. 10s. 6d.

JORDAN (William Leighton).—THE STANDARD OF VALUE. 8vo. 6s.

JUSTINIAN.—THE INSTITUTES OF JUSTINIAN; Latin Text, with English Introduction, &c. By THOMAS C. SANDARS. 8vo. 18s.

KALISCH (M. M.).—BIBLE STUDIES. Part I. The Prophecies of Balaam. 8vo. 10s. 6d. Part II. The Book of Jonah. 8vo. 10s. 6d.

KALISCH (M. M.).—COMMENTARY ON THE OLD TESTAMENT; with a New Translation. Vol. I. Genesis, 8vo. 18s., or adapted for the General Reader, 12s. Vol. II. Exodus, 15s., or adapted for the General Reader, 12s. Vol. III. Leviticus, Part I. 15s., or adapted for the General Reader, 8s. Vol. IV. Leviticus, Part II. 15s., or adapted for the General Reader, 8s.

KANT (Immanuel).—CRITIQUE OF PRACTICAL REASON, AND OTHER WORKS ON THE THEORY OF ETHICS. 8vo. 12s. 6d.

——— INTRODUCTION TO LOGIC. Translated by T. K. Abbott. Notes by S. T. Coleridge. 8vo. 6s.

KENNEDY (Arthur Clark).—PICTURES IN RHYME. With 4 Illustrations by Maurice Greiffenhagen. Crown 8vo. 6s.

KILLICK (Rev. A. H.).—HANDBOOK TO MILL'S SYSTEM OF LOGIC. Crown 8vo. 3s. 6d.

KNIGHT (E. F.).—THE CRUISE OF THE 'ALERTE'; the Narrative of a Search for Treasure on the Desert Island of Trinidad. With 2 Maps and 23 Illustrations. Crown 8vo. 10s. 6d.

——— SAVE ME FROM MY FRIENDS: a Novel. Crown 8vo. 6s.

LADD (George T.).—ELEMENTS OF PHYSIOLOGICAL PSYCHOLOGY. 8vo. 21s.

——— OUTLINES OF PHYSIOLOGICAL PSYCHOLOGY. A Text-Book of Mental Science for Academies and Colleges. 8vo. 12s.

LANG (Andrew).—CUSTOM AND MYTH: Studies of Early Usage and Belief. With 15 Illustrations. Crown 8vo. 7s. 6d.

——— BOOKS AND BOOKMEN. With 2 Coloured Plates and 17 Illustrations. Crown 8vo. 6s. 6d.

——— GRASS OF PARNASSUS. A Volume of Selected Verses. Fcp. 8vo. 6s.

——— BALLADS OF BOOKS. Edited by ANDREW LANG. Fcp. 8vo. 6s.

——— THE BLUE FAIRY BOOK. Edited by ANDREW LANG. With 8 Plates and 130 Illustrations in the Text. Crown 8vo. 6s.

——— THE RED FAIRY BOOK. Edited by ANDREW LANG. With 4 Plates and 96 Illustrations in the Text. Crown 8vo. 6s.

——— THE BLUE POETRY BOOK. With 12 Plates and 88 Illustrations in the Text. Crown 8vo. 6s.

——— ANGLING SKETCHES. With Illustrations by W. G. BURN-MURDOCH. Crown 8vo. 7s. 6d.

LAVISSE (Ernest).—GENERAL VIEW OF THE POLITICAL HISTORY OF EUROPE.

LAYARD (Nina F.).—POEMS. Crown 8vo. 6s.

LECKY (W. E. H.).—HISTORY OF ENGLAND IN THE EIGHTEENTH CENTURY. 8vo. Vols. I. and II. 1700-1760. 36s. Vols. III. and IV. 1760-1784. 36s. Vols. V. and VI. 1784-1793. 36s. Vols. VII. and VIII. 1793-1800. 36s.

———— THE HISTORY OF EUROPEAN MORALS FROM AUGUSTUS TO CHARLEMAGNE. 2 vols. Crown 8vo. 16s.

———— HISTORY OF THE RISE AND INFLUENCE OF THE SPIRIT OF RATIONALISM IN EUROPE. 2 vols. Crown 8vo. 16s.

———— POEMS. Fcap. 8vo. 5s.

LEES (J. A.) and CLUTTERBUCK (W. J.).—B.C. 1887, A RAMBLE IN BRITISH COLUMBIA. With Map and 75 Illustrations. Cr. 8vo. 6s.

LEGER (Louis).—A HISTORY OF AUSTRO-HUNGARY. From the Earliest Time to the year 1889. With Preface by E. A. Freeman. Cr. 8vo. 10s. 6d.

LEWES (George Henry).—THE HISTORY OF PHILOSOPHY, from Thales to Comte. 2 vols. 8vo. 32s.

LIDDELL (Colonel R. T.).—MEMOIRS OF THE TENTH ROYAL HUSSARS. With Numerous Illustrations. 2 vols. Imperial 8vo. 63s.

LONGMAN (Frederick W.).—CHESS OPENINGS. Fcp. 8vo. 2s. 6d.

———— FREDERICK THE GREAT AND THE SEVEN YEARS' WAR. Fcp. 8vo. 2s. 6d.

LONGMORE (Sir T.).—RICHARD WISEMAN, Surgeon and Sergeant-Surgeon to Charles II. A Biographical Study. With Portrait.

LOUDON (J. C.).—ENCYCLOPÆDIA OF GARDENING. With 1000 Woodcuts. 8vo. 21s.

———— ENCYCLOPÆDIA OF AGRICULTURE; the Laying-out, Improvement, and Management of Landed Property. With 1100 Woodcuts. 8vo. 21s.

———— ENCYCLOPÆDIA OF PLANTS; the Specific Character, &c., of all Plants found in Great Britain. With 12,000 Woodcuts. 8vo. 42s.

LUBBOCK (Sir J.).—THE ORIGIN OF CIVILISATION and the Primitive Condition of Man. With 5 Plates and 20 Illustrations in the Text. 8vo. 18s.

LYALL (Edna).—THE AUTOBIOGRAPHY OF A SLANDER. Fcp. 8vo. 1s. sewed.

LYDE (Lionel W.).—AN INTRODUCTION TO ANCIENT HISTORY. With 3 Coloured Maps. Crown 8vo. 3s.

MACAULAY (Lord).—COMPLETE WORKS OF LORD MACAULAY. Library Edition, 8 vols. 8vo. £5 5s. | Cabinet Edition, 16 vols. post 8vo. £4 16s.

———— HISTORY OF ENGLAND FROM THE ACCESSION OF JAMES THE SECOND.
Popular Edition, 2 vols. Crown 8vo. 5s. | People's Edition, 4 vols. Crown 8vo. 16s.
Student's Edition, 2 vols. Crown 8vo. 12s. | Cabinet Edition, 8 vols. Post 8vo. 48s.
Library Edition, 5 vols. 8vo. £4

———— CRITICAL AND HISTORICAL ESSAYS, WITH LAYS OF ANCIENT ROME, in 1 volume.
Popular Edition, Crown 8vo. 2s. 6d. | Authorised Edition, Crown 8vo. 2s. 6d., or 3s. 6d. gilt edges.

[*Continued.*

MACAULAY (Lord).—ESSAYS *(continued)*.

——— CRITICAL AND HISTORICAL ESSAYS.

Student's Edition.   Crown 8vo. 6s. | Trevelyan Edition, 2 vols. Crown 8vo. 9s.
People's Edition, 2 vols. Crown 8vo. 8s. | Cabinet Edition, 4 vols. Post 8vo. 24s.
 | Library Edition, 3 vols. 8vo. 36s.

——— ESSAYS which may be had separately, price 6d. each sewed.   1s. each cloth.

Addison and Walpole. | Ranke and Gladstone.
Frederic the Great. | Milton and Machiavelli.
Croker's Boswell's Johnson. | Lord Bacon.
Hallam's Constitutional History. | Lord Clive.
Warren Hastings (3d. sewed, 6d. cloth). | Lord Byron, and the Comic Drama-
The Earl of Chatham (Two Essays). | tists of the Restoration.

The Essay on Warren Hastings, anno- | The Essay on Lord Clive, annotated by
tated by S. Hales. Fcp. 8vo. 1s. 6d. | H. Courthope Bowen. Fcp. 8vo. 2s. 6d.

——— SPEECHES.   People's Edition, Crown 8vo. 3s. 6d.

——— LAYS OF ANCIENT ROME, &c.   Illustrated by G. Scharf.   Library
Edition. Fcp. 4to. 10s. 6d.

Bijou Edition, 18mo. 2s. 6d. gilt top. | Popular Edition, Fcp. 4to. 6d. sewed,
 | 1s. cloth.

——————————————————— | Illustrated by J. R. Weguelin.   Crown
8vo. 3s. 6d. gilt edges. |

——————————————— | Annotated Edition, Fcp. 8vo. 1s. sewed,
Cabinet Edition, Post 8vo. 3s. 6d. | 1s. 6d. cloth.

——— MISCELLANEOUS WRITINGS.

People's Edition.   Crown 8vo. 4s. 6d. | Library Edition, 2 vols. 8vo. 21s.

——— MISCELLANEOUS WRITINGS AND SPEECHES.

Popular Edition.   Crown 8vo. 2s. 6d. | Cabinet Edition, Post 8vo. 24s.
Student's Edition.   Crown 8vo. 6s. |

——— SELECTIONS FROM THE WRITINGS OF LORD MACAULAY.
Edited, with Notes, by the Right Hon. Sir G. O. TREVELYAN. Crown 8vo. 6s.

——— THE LIFE AND LETTERS OF LORD MACAULAY.   By the Right
Hon. Sir G. O. TREVELYAN.

Popular Edition.   Crown. 8vo. 2s. 6d. | Cabinet Edition, 2 vols. Post 8vo. 12s.
Student's Edition.   Crown 8vo. 6s. | Library Edition, 2 vols. 8vo. 36s.

MACDONALD (George).—UNSPOKEN SERMONS.   Three Series.
Crown 8vo. 3s. 6d. each.

——— THE MIRACLES OF OUR LORD.   Crown 8vo. 3s. 6d.

——— A BOOK OF STRIFE, IN THE FORM OF THE DIARY OF AN
OLD SOUL : Poems. 12mo. 6s.

MACFARREN (Sir G. A.).—LECTURES ON HARMONY.   8vo. 12s.

——— ADDRESSES AND LECTURES.   Crown 8vo. 6s. 6d.

MACKAIL (J. W.).—SELECT EPIGRAMS FROM THE GREEK AN-
THOLOGY. With a Revised Text, Introduction, Translation, &c. 8vo. 16s.

MACLEOD (Henry D.).—THE ELEMENTS OF BANKING.   Crown
8vo. 3s. 6d.

——— THE THEORY AND PRACTICE OF BANKING.   Vol. I. 8vo. 12s.,
Vol. II. 14s.

——— THE THEORY OF CREDIT.   8vo.   Vol. I. [*New Edition in the Press*] ;
Vol. II. Part I. 4s. 6d. ; Vol. II. Part II. 10s. 6d.

McCULLOCH (J. R.).—THE DICTIONARY OF COMMERCE and Commercial Navigation. With 11 Maps and 30 Charts. 8vo. 63s.

MACVINE (John).—SIXTY-THREE YEARS' ANGLING, from the Mountain Streamlet to the Mighty Tay. Crown 8vo. 10s. 6d.

MALMESBURY (The Earl of).—MEMOIRS OF AN EX-MINISTER. Crown 8vo. 7s. 6d.

MANNERING (G. E.).—WITH AXE AND ROPE IN THE NEW ZEALAND ALPS. Illustrated. 8vo. 12s. 6d.

MANUALS OF CATHOLIC PHILOSOPHY (*Stonyhurst Series*).

Logic. By Richard F. Clarke. Crown 8vo. 5s.

First Principles of Knowledge. By John Rickaby. Crown 8vo. 5s.

Moral Philosophy (Ethics and Natural Law). By Joseph Rickaby. Crown 8vo. 5s.

General Metaphysics. By John Rickaby. Crown 8vo. 5s.

Psychology. By Michael Maher. Crown 8vo. 6s. 6d.

Natural Theology. By Bernard Boedder. Crown 8vo. 6s. 6d.

A Manual of Political Economy. By C. S. Devas. 6s. 6d. [*In preparation.*

MARTINEAU (James).—HOURS OF THOUGHT ON SACRED THINGS. Two Volumes of Sermons. 2 vols. Crown 8vo. 7s. 6d. each.

———— ENDEAVOURS AFTER THE CHRISTIAN LIFE. Discourses. Crown 8vo. 7s. 6d.

———— THE SEAT OF AUTHORITY IN RELIGION. 8vo. 14s.

———— ESSAYS, REVIEWS, AND ADDRESSES. 4 vols. Crown 8vo. 7s. 6d. each.

I. **Personal : Political.**

II. **Ecclesiastical : Historical.**

III. **Theological : Philosophical.**

IV. **Academical : Religious.**

MASON (Agnes).—THE STEPS OF THE SUN : Daily Readings of Prose. 16mo. 3s. 6d.

MAUNDER'S TREASURIES. Fcp. 8vo. 6s. each volume.

Biographical Treasury.

Treasury of Natural History. With 900 Woodcuts.

Treasury of Geography. With 7 Maps and 16 Plates.

Scientific and Literary Treasury.

Historical Treasury.

Treasury of Knowledge.

The Treasury of Bible Knowledge. By the Rev. J. AYRE. With 5 Maps, 15 Plates, and 300 Woodcuts. Fcp. 8vo. 6s.

The Treasury of Botany. Edited by J. LINDLEY and T. MOORE. With 274 Woodcuts and 20 Steel Plates. 2 vols.

MATTHEWS (Brander).—A FAMILY TREE, and other Stories. Crown 8vo. 6s.

———— PEN AND INK—School Papers. Crown 8vo. 5s.

———— WITH MY FRIENDS : Tales told in Partnership. Crown 8vo. 6s.

MAX MÜLLER (F.).—SELECTED ESSAYS ON LANGUAGE, MYTHOLOGY, AND RELIGION. 2 vols. Crown 8vo. 16s.

———— THREE LECTURES ON THE SCIENCE OF LANGUAGE. Cr. 8vo. 3s.

———— THE SCIENCE OF LANGUAGE, founded on Lectures delivered at the Royal Institution in 1861 and 1863. 2 vols. Crown 8vo. 21s.

———— HIBBERT LECTURES ON THE ORIGIN AND GROWTH OF RELIGION, as illustrated by the Religions of India. Crown 8vo. 7s. 6d.

[*Continued.*

MAX MÜLLER (F.)—INTRODUCTION TO THE SCIENCE OF RELIGION; Four Lectures delivered at the Royal Institution. Crown 8vo. 7s. 6d.

———— NATURAL RELIGION. The Gifford Lectures, delivered before the University of Glasgow in 1888. Crown 8vo. 10s. 6d.

———— PHYSICAL RELIGION. The Gifford Lectures, delivered before the University of Glasgow in 1890. Crown 8vo. 10s. 6d.

———— THE SCIENCE OF THOUGHT. 8vo. 21s.

———— THREE INTRODUCTORY LECTURES ON THE SCIENCE OF THOUGHT. 8vo. 2s. 6d.

———— BIOGRAPHIES OF WORDS, AND THE HOME OF THE ARYAS. Crown 8vo. 7s. 6d.

———— A SANSKRIT GRAMMAR FOR BEGINNERS. New and Abridged Edition. By A. A. MacDonell. Crown 8vo. 6s.

MAY (Sir Thomas Erskine).—THE CONSTITUTIONAL HISTORY OF ENGLAND since the Accession of George III. 3 vols. Crown 8vo. 18s.

MEADE (L. T.).—THE O'DONNELLS OF INCHFAWN. Crown 8vo. 6s.

———— DADDY'S BOY. With Illustrations. Crown 8vo. 5s.

———— DEB AND THE DUCHESS. Illustrated by M. E. Edwards. Cr. 8vo. 5s.

———— HOUSE OF SURPRISES. Illustrated by E. M. Scannell. Cr. 8vo. 3s. 6d.

———— THE BERESFORD PRIZE. Illustrated by M. E. Edwards. Cr. 8vo. 5s.

MEATH (The Earl of).—SOCIAL ARROWS: Reprinted Articles on various Social Subjects. Crown 8vo. 5s.

———— PROSPERITY OR PAUPERISM? Physical, Industrial, and Technical Training. Edited by the Earl of Meath. 8vo. 5s.

MELVILLE (G. J. Whyte).—Novels by. Crown 8vo. 1s. each, boards; 1s. 6d. each, cloth.

The Gladiators.	The Queen's Maries.	Digby Grand.
The Interpreter.	Holmby House.	General Bounce.
Good for Nothing.	Kate Coventry.	

MENDELSSOHN.—THE LETTERS OF FELIX MENDELSSOHN. Translated by Lady Wallace. 2 vols. Crown 8vo. 10s.

MERIVALE (Rev. Chas.).—HISTORY OF THE ROMANS UNDER THE EMPIRE. Cabinet Edition, 8 vols. Crown 8vo. 48s. Popular Edition, 8 vols. Crown 8vo. 3s. 6d. each.

———— THE FALL OF THE ROMAN REPUBLIC: a Short History of the Last Century of the Commonwealth. 12mo. 7s. 6d.

———— GENERAL HISTORY OF ROME FROM B.C. 753 TO A.D. 476. Cr. 8vo. 7s. 6d.

———— THE ROMAN TRIUMVIRATES. With Maps. Fcp. 8vo. 2s. 6d.

MILES (W. A.).—THE CORRESPONDENCE OF WILLIAM AUGUSTUS MILES ON THE FRENCH REVOLUTION, 1789-1817. 2 vols. 8vo. 32s.

MILL (James).—ANALYSIS OF THE PHENOMENA OF THE HUMAN MIND. 2 vols. 8vo. 28s.

MILL (John Stuart).—PRINCIPLES OF POLITICAL ECONOMY. Library Edition, 2 vols. 8vo. 30s. | People's Edition, 1 vol. Crown 8vo. 3s. 6d.

———— A SYSTEM OF LOGIC. Crown 8vo. 3s. 6d.

———— ON LIBERTY. Crown 8vo. 1s. 4d. [*Continued.*

MILL (J. S.).—ON REPRESENTATIVE GOVERNMENT. Crown 8vo. 2s.

———— UTILITARIANISM. 8vo. 5s.

———— EXAMINATION OF SIR WILLIAM HAMILTON'S PHILO-SOPHY. 8vo. 16s.

———— NATURE, THE UTILITY OF RELIGION AND THEISM. Three Essays, 8vo. 5s.

MOLESWORTH (Mrs.).—MARRYING AND GIVING IN MARRIAGE: a Novel. Fcp. 8vo. 2s. 6d.

———— SILVERTHORNS. With Illustrations by F. Noel Paton. Cr. 8vo. 5s.

———— THE PALACE IN THE GARDEN. With Illustrations. Cr. 8vo. 5s.

———— THE THIRD MISS ST. QUENTIN. Crown 8vo. 6s.

———— NEIGHBOURS. With Illustrations by M. Ellen Edwards. Cr. 8vo. 6s.

———— THE STORY OF A SPRING MORNING. With Illustrations. Cr.8vo. 5s.

MOORE (Edward).—DANTE AND HIS EARLY BIOGRAPHERS. Crown 8vo. 4s. 6d.

MULHALL (Michael G.).—HISTORY OF PRICES SINCE THE YEAR 1850. Crown 8vo. 6s.

MURRAY (David Christie and Henry).—A DANGEROUS CATS-PAW: a Story. Crown 8vo. 2s. 6d.

MURRAY (Christie) and HERMAN (Henry).—WILD DARRIE: a Story. Crown 8vo. 2s. boards; 2s. 6d. cloth.

NANSEN (Dr. Fridtjof).—THE FIRST CROSSING OF GREENLAND. With 5 Maps, 12 Plates, and 150 Illustrations in the Text. 2 vols. 8vo. 36s.

NAPIER.—THE LIFE OF SIR JOSEPH NAPIER, BART., EX-LORD CHANCELLOR OF IRELAND. By ALEX. CHARLES EWALD. 8vo. 15s.

———— THE LECTURES, ESSAYS, AND LETTERS OF THE RIGHT HON. SIR JOSEPH NAPIER, BART. 8vo. 12s. 6d.

NESBIT (E.).—LEAVES OF LIFE: Verses. Crown 8vo. 5s.

NEWMAN.—THE LETTERS AND CORRESPONDENCE OF JOHN HENRY NEWMAN during his Life in the English Church. With a brief Autobiographical Memoir. Edited by Anne Mozley. With Portraits, 2 vols. 8vo. 30s. *net.*

NEWMAN (Cardinal).—Works by:—

Sermons to Mixed Congregations. Crown 8vo. 6s.

Sermons on Various Occasions. Cr. 8vo. 6s.

The Idea of a University defined and illustrated. Cabinet Edition, Cr. 8vo. 7s. Cheap Edition, Cr. 8vo. 3s. 6d.

Historical Sketches. Cabinet Edition, 3 vols. Crown 8vo. 6s. each. Cheap Edition, 3 vols. Cr. 8vo. 3s. 6d. each.

The Arians of the Fourth Century. Cabinet Edition, Crown 8vo. 6s. Cheap Edition, Crown 8vo. 3s. 6d.

Select Treatises of St. Athanasius in Controversy with the Arians. Freely Translated. 2 vols. Cr. 8vo. 15s.

Discussions and Arguments on Various Subjects. Cabinet Edition, Crown 8vo. 6s. Cheap Edition, Crown 8vo. 3s. 6d.

[*Continued.*

NEWMAN (Cardinal).—Works by :—(continued).

Apologia Pro Vita Sua. Cabinet Ed., Crown 8vo. 6s. Cheap Ed. 3s. 6d.

Development of Christian Doctrine. Cabinet Edition, Crown 8vo. 6s. Cheap Edition, Cr. 8vo. 3s. 6d.

Certain Difficulties felt by Anglicans in Catholic Teaching Considered. Cabinet Edition. Vol. I. Crown 8vo. 7s. 6d. ; Vol. II. Crown 8vo. 5s. 6d. Cheap Edition, 2 vols. Crown 8vo. 3s. 6d. each.

The Via Media of the Anglican Church, Illustrated in Lectures, &c. Cabinet Edition, 2 vols. Cr. 8vo. 6s. each. Cheap Edition, 2 vols. Crown 8vo. 3s. 6d. each.

Essays, Critical and Historical. Cabinet Edition, 2 vols. Crown 8vo. 12s. Cheap Edition, 2 vols. Cr. 8vo. 7s.

Biblical and Ecclesiastical Miracles. Cabinet Edition, Crown 8vo. 6s. Cheap Edition, Crown 8vo. 3s. 6d.

Present Position of Catholics in England. Crown 8vo. 7s. 6d.

Tracts. 1. Dissertatiunculae. 2. On the Text of the Seven Epistles of St. Ignatius. 3. Doctrinal Causes of Arianism. 4. Apollinarianism. 5. St. Cyril's Formula. 6. Ordo de Tempore. 7. Douay Version of Scripture. Crown 8vo. 8s.

An Essay in Aid of a Grammar of Assent. Cabinet Edition, Crown 8vo. 7s. 6d. Cheap Edition, Crown 8vo. 3s. 6d.

Callista : a Tale of the Third Century. Cabinet Edition, Crown 8vo. 6s. Cheap Edition, Crown 8vo. 3s. 6d.

Loss and Gain : a Tale. Cabinet Edition, Crown 8vo. 6s. Cheap Edition, Crown 8vo. 3s. 6d.

The Dream of Gerontius. 16mo. 6d. sewed, 1s. cloth.

Verses on Various Occasions. Cabinet Edition, Crown 8vo. 6s. Cheap Edition, Crown 8vo. 3s. 6d.

*** *For Cardinal Newman's other Works see Messrs. Longmans & Co.'s Catalogue of Theological Works.*

NORRIS (W. E.).—MRS. FENTON : a Sketch.   Crown 8vo. 6s.

NORTON (Charles L.).—POLITICAL AMERICANISMS : a Glossary of Terms and Phrases Current in American Politics.   Crown 8vo. 2s. 6d.

———— A HANDBOOK OF FLORIDA.   49 Maps and Plans.   Fcp. 8vo. 5s.

NORTHCOTE (W. H.).—LATHES AND TURNING, Simple, Mechanical, and Ornamental.   With 338 Illustrations.   8vo. 18s.

O'BRIEN (William).—WHEN WE WERE BOYS: A Novel.   Cr. 8vo. 2s. 6d.

OLIPHANT (Mrs.).—MADAM.   Crown 8vo. 1s. boards ; 1s. 6d. cloth.

———— IN TRUST.   Crown 8vo. 1s. boards ; 1s. 6d. cloth.

———— LADY CAR : the Sequel of a Life.   Crown 8vo. 2s. 6d.

OMAN (C. W. C.).—A HISTORY OF GREECE FROM THE EARLIEST TIMES TO THE MACEDONIAN CONQUEST.   With Maps.   Cr. 8vo. 4s. 6d.

O'REILLY (Mrs.).—HURSTLEIGH DENE : a Tale.   Crown 8vo. 5s.

PAUL (Hermann).—PRINCIPLES OF THE HISTORY OF LANGUAGE. Translated by H. A. Strong.   8vo. 10s. 6d.

PAYN (James).—THE LUCK OF THE DARRELLS.   Cr. 8vo. 1s. bds. ; 1s. 6d. cl.

———— THICKER THAN WATER.   Crown 8vo. 1s. boards ; 1s. 6d. cloth.

PERRING (Sir Philip).—HARD KNOTS IN SHAKESPEARE. 8vo. 7s. 6d.

———— THE 'WORKS AND DAYS' OF MOSES.   Crown 8vo. 3s. 6d.

PHILLIPPS-WOLLEY (C.).—SNAP : a Legend of the Lone Mountain. With 13 Illustrations by H. G. Willink. Crown 8vo. 6s.

POLE (W.).—THE THEORY OF THE MODERN SCIENTIFIC GAME OF WHIST. Fcp. 8vo. 2s. 6d.

POLLOCK (W. H. and Lady).—THE SEAL OF FATE. Cr. 8vo. 6s.

POOLE (W. H. and Mrs.).—COOKERY FOR THE DIABETIC. Fcp. 8vo. 2s. 6d.

PRENDERGAST (John P.).—IRELAND, FROM THE RESTORATION TO THE REVOLUTION, 1660-1690. 8vo. 5s.

PROCTOR (R.A.).—Works by :—

Old and New Astronomy. 12 Parts, 2s. 6d. each. Supplementary Section, 1s. Complete in 1 vol. 4to. 36s. [*In course of publication.*]

The Orbs Around Us. Crown 8vo. 5s.

Other Worlds than Ours. With 14 Illustrations. Crown 8vo. 5s.

The Moon. Crown 8vo. 5s.

Universe of Stars. 8vo. 10s. 6d.

Larger Star Atlas for the Library, in 12 Circular Maps, with Introduction and 2 Index Pages. Folio, 15s. or Maps only, 12s. 6d.

The Student's Atlas. In 12 Circular Maps. 8vo. 5s.

New Star Atlas. In 12 Circular Maps. Crown 8vo. 5s.

Light Science for Leisure Hours. 3 vols. Crown 8vo. 5s. each.

Chance and Luck. Crown 8vo. 2s. boards ; 2s. 6d. cloth.

Pleasant Ways in Science. Cr. 8vo. 5s.

How to Play Whist : with the Laws and Etiquette of Whist. Crown 8vo. 3s. 6d.

Home Whist : an Easy Guide to Correct Play. 16mo. 1s.

Studies of Venus-Transits. With 7 Diagrams and 10 Plates. 8vo. 5s.

The Stars in their Season. 12 Maps. Royal 8vo. 5s.

Star Primer. Showing the Starry Sky Week by Week, in 24 Hourly Maps. Crown 4to. 2s. 6d.

The Seasons Pictured in 48 Sun-Views of the Earth, and 24 Zodiacal Maps, &c. Demy 4to. 5s.

Strength and Happiness. With 9 Illustrations. Crown 8vo. 5s.

Strength : How to get Strong and keep Strong. Crown 8vo. 2s.

Rough Ways Made Smooth. Essays on Scientific Subjects. Crown 8vo. 5s.

Our Place among Infinities. Cr. 8vo. 5s.

The Expanse of Heaven. Cr. 8vo. 5s.

The Great Pyramid. Crown 8vo. 5s.

Myths and Marvels of Astronomy Crown 8vo. 5s.

Nature Studies. By Grant Allen, A. Wilson, T. Foster, E. Clodd, and R. A. Proctor. Crown 8vo. 5s.

Leisure Readings. By E. Clodd, A. Wilson, T. Foster, A. C. Ranyard, and R. A. Proctor. Crown 8vo. 5s.

PRYCE (John).—THE ANCIENT BRITISH CHURCH : an Historical Essay. Crown 8vo. 6s.

RANSOME (Cyril).—THE RISE OF CONSTITUTIONAL GOVERNMENT IN ENGLAND : being a Series of Twenty Lectures. Crown 8vo. 6s.

RAWLINSON (Canon G.).—THE HISTORY OF PHŒNICIA. 8vo. 24s.

RENDLE (William) and NORMAN (Philip).—THE INNS OF OLD SOUTHWARK, and their Associations. With Illustrations. Royal 8vo. 28s.

RIBOT (Th.).—THE PSYCHOLOGY OF ATTENTION. Crown 8vo. 3s.

RICH (A.).—A DICTIONARY OF ROMAN AND GREEK ANTIQUITIES. With 2000 Woodcuts. Crown 8vo. 7s. 6d.

RICHARDSON (Dr. B. W.).—NATIONAL HEALTH. A Review. of the Works of Sir Edwin Chadwick, K.C.B. Crown 4s. 6d.

RILEY (Athelstan).—ATHOS; or, The Mountain of the Monks. With Map and 29 Illustrations. 8vo. 21s.

ROBERTS (Alexander).—GREEK THE LANGUAGE OF CHRIST AND HIS APOSTLES. 8vo. 18s.

ROCKHILL (W. W.).—THE LAND OF THE LAMAS: Notes of a Journey through China, Mongolia, and Tibet. With Maps and Illustrations. 8vo. 15s.

ROGET (John Lewis).—A HISTORY OF THE 'OLD WATER COLOUR' SOCIETY. 2 vols. Royal 8vo. 42s.

ROGET (Peter M.).—THESAURUS OF ENGLISH WORDS AND PHRASES. Crown 8vo. 10s. 6d.

RONALDS (Alfred).—THE FLY-FISHER'S ETYMOLOGY. With 20 Coloured Plates. 8vo. 14s.

ROSSETTI (Maria Francesca).—A SHADOW OF DANTE: being an Essay towards studying Himself, his World, and his Pilgrimage. Cr. 8vo. 10s. 6d.

RUSSELL.—A LIFE OF LORD JOHN RUSSELL. By SPENCER WALPOLE. 2 vols. 8vo. 36s. Cabinet Edition, 2 vols. Crown 8vo. 12s.

SEEBOHM (Frederick). — THE OXFORD REFORMERS — JOHN COLET, ERASMUS, AND THOMAS MORE. 8vo. 14s.

———— THE ENGLISH VILLAGE COMMUNITY Examined in its Relations to the Manorial and Tribal Systems, &c. 13 Maps and Plates. 8vo. 16s.

———— THE ERA OF THE PROTESTANT REVOLUTION. With Map. Fcp. 8vo. 2s. 6d.

SEWELL (Elizabeth M.).—STORIES AND TALES. Crown 8vo. 1s. 6d each, cloth plain; 2s. 6d. each, cloth extra, gilt edges :—

Amy Herbert.	Katharine Ashton.	Gertrude.
The Earl's Daughter.	Margaret Percival.	Ivors.
The Experience of Life.	Laneton Parsonage.	Home Life.
A Glimpse of the World.	Ursula.	After Life.
Cleve Hall.		

SHAKESPEARE.—BOWDLER'S FAMILY SHAKESPEARE. 1 vol. 8vo. With 36 Woodcuts, 14s., or in 6 vols. Fcp. 8vo. 21s.

———— OUTLINE OF THE LIFE OF SHAKESPEARE. By J. O. HALLIWELL-PHILLIPPS. 2 vols. Royal 8vo. £1 1s.

———— SHAKESPEARE'S TRUE LIFE. By JAMES WALTER. With 500 Illustrations. Imp. 8vo. 21s.

———— THE SHAKESPEARE BIRTHDAY BOOK. By MARY F. DUNBAR. 32mo. 1s. 6d. cloth. With Photographs, 32mo. 5s. Drawing-Room Edition, with Photographs, Fcp. 8vo. 10s. 6d.

SHORT (T. V.).—SKETCH OF THE HISTORY OF THE CHURCH OF ENGLAND to the Revolution of 1688. Crown 8vo. 7s. 6d.

SILVER LIBRARY, The.—Crown 8vo. price 3s. 6d. each volume.

BAKER'S (Sir S. W.) Eight Years in Ceylon. With 6 Illustrations.

———— **Rifle and Hound in Ceylon.** With 6 Illustrations.

BRASSEY'S (Lady) A Voyage in the 'Sunbeam'. With 66 Illustrations.

CLODD'S (E.) Story of Creation: a Plain Account of Evolution. With 77 Illustrations.

DOYLE'S (A. Conan) Micah Clarke: a Tale of Monmouth's Rebellion.

FROUDE'S (J. A.) Short Studies on Great Subjects. 4 vols.

———— **Cæsar:** a Sketch.

———— **Thomas Carlyle:** a History of his Life. 1795-1835. 2 vols. 1834-1881. 2 vols.

———— **The Two Chiefs of Dunboy:** an Irish Romance of the Last Century.

GLEIG'S (Rev. G. R.) Life of the Duke of Wellington. With Portrait.

HAGGARD'S (H. R.) She: A History of Adventure. 32 Illustrations.

———— **Allan Quatermain.** With 20 Illustrations.

———— **Colonel Quaritch, V.C.:** a Tale of Country Life.

———— **Cleopatra.** With 29 Full-page Illustrations.

HOWITT'S (W.) Visits to Remarkable Places. 80 Illustrations.

JEFFERIES' (R.) The Story of My Heart: My Autobiography. With Portrait.

———— **Field and Hedgerow.** Last Essays of. With Portrait.

MACLEOD'S (H. D.) The Elements of Banking.

MARSHMAN'S (J. C.) Memoirs of Sir Henry Havelock.

MERIVALE'S (Dean) History of the Romans under the Empire. 8 vols.

MILL'S (J. S.) Principles of Political Economy.

———— **System of Logic.**

NEWMAN'S (Cardinal) Historical Sketches. 3 vols.

———— **Apologia Pro Vita Sua.**

———— **Callista:** a Tale of the Third Century.

———— **Loss and Gain:** a Tale.

———— **Essays, Critical and Historical.** 2 vols.

———— **An Essay on the Development of Christian Doctrine.**

———— **The Arians of the Fourth Century.**

———— **Verses on Various Occasions.**

———— **Parochial and Plain Sermons.** 8 vols.

———— **Selection, adapted to the Seasons of the Ecclesiastical Year,** from the 'Parochial and Plain Sermons'.

———— **Difficulties felt by Anglicans in Catholic Teaching Considered.** 2 vols.

———— **The Idea of a University** defined and Illustrated.

———— **Biblical and Ecclesiastical Miracles.**

———— **Discussions and Arguments on Various Subjects.**

———— **Grammar of Assent.**

———— **The Via Media of the Anglican Church,** illustrated in Lectures, &c. 2 vols.

———— **Sermons bearing upon Subjects of the Day.** Edited by the Rev. J. W. Copeland, B.D., late Rector of Farnham, Essex.

STANLEY'S (Bishop) Familiar History of Birds. With 160 Illustrations.

WOOD'S (Rev. J. G.) Petland Revisited. With 33 Illustrations.

———— **Strange Dwellings.** With 60 Illustrations.

———— **Out of Doors.** With 11 Illustrations.

SMITH (R. Bosworth).—CARTHAGE AND THE CARTHAGINIANS. Maps, Plans, &c. Crown 8vo. 6s.

SOPHOCLES. Translated into English Verse. By ROBERT WHITELAW. Crown 8vo. 8s. 6d.

STANLEY (E.).—A FAMILIAR HISTORY OF BIRDS. With 160 Woodcuts. Crown 8vo. 3s. 6d.

STEEL (J. H.).—A TREATISE ON THE DISEASES OF THE DOG; being a Manual of Canine Pathology. 88 Illustrations. 8vo. 10s. 6d.

———— A TREATISE ON THE DISEASES OF THE OX; being a Manual of Bovine Pathology. 2 Plates and 117 Woodcuts. 8vo. 15s.

———— A TREATISE ON THE DISEASES OF THE SHEEP; being a Manual of Ovine Pathology. With Coloured Plate and 99 Woodcuts. 8vo. 12s.

STEPHEN (Sir James).— ESSAYS IN ECCLESIASTICAL BIO-GRAPHY. Crown 8vo. 7s. 6d.

STEPHENS (H. Morse).—A HISTORY OF THE FRENCH REVOLUTION. 3 vols. 8vo. Vol. I. 18s. Vol. II. 18s.   [*Vol. III. in the press.*

STEVENSON (Robt. Louis).—A CHILD'S GARDEN OF VERSES. Small Fcp. 8vo. 5s.

———— THE DYNAMITER. Fcp. 8vo. 1s. sewed, 1s. 6d. cloth.

———— STRANGE CASE OF DR. JEKYLL AND MR. HYDE. Fcp. 8vo. 1s. sewed, 1s. 6d. cloth.

STEVENSON (Robert Louis) and OSBOURNE (Lloyd).—THE WRONG BOX. Crown 8vo. 5s.

STOCK (St. George).—DEDUCTIVE LOGIC. Fcp. 8vo. 3s. 6d.

'STONEHENGE.'—THE DOG IN HEALTH AND DISEASE. With 84 Wood Engravings. Square Crown 8vo. 7s. 6d.

STRONG (Herbert A.), LOGEMAN (Willem S.) and WHEELER (B. I.).—INTRODUCTION TO THE STUDY OF THE HISTORY OF LANGUAGE. 8vo. 10s. 6d.

SUPERNATURAL RELIGION; an Inquiry into the Reality of Divine Revelation. 3 vols. 8vo. 36s.

REPLY (A) TO DR. LIGHTFOOT'S ESSAYS. By the Author of 'Supernatural Religion'. 8vo. 6s.

STUTFIELD (H.).—THE BRETHREN OF MOUNT ATLAS: being the First Part of an African Theosophical Story. Crown 8vo. 6s.

SYMES (J. E.).—PRELUDE TO MODERN HISTORY: being a Brief Sketch of the World's History from the Third to the Ninth Century. With 5 Maps. Crown 8vo. 2s. 6d.

TAYLOR (Colonel Meadows).—A STUDENT'S MANUAL OF THE HISTORY OF INDIA, from the Earliest Period to the Present Time. Crown 8vo. 7s. 6d.

THOMPSON (D. Greenleaf).—THE PROBLEM OF EVIL: an Introduction to the Practical Sciences. 8vo. 10s. 6d.

———— A SYSTEM OF PSYCHOLOGY. 2 vols. 8vo. 36s.

———— THE RELIGIOUS SENTIMENTS OF THE HUMAN MIND. 8vo. 7s. 6d.

———— SOCIAL PROGRESS: an Essay. 8vo. 7s. 6d.

———— THE PHILOSOPHY OF FICTION IN LITERATURE: an Essay. Crown 8vo. 6s.

THREE IN NORWAY. By Two of THEM. With a Map and 59 Illustrations. Crown 8vo. 2s. boards; 2s. 6d. cloth.

TOYNBEE (Arnold).—LECTURES ON THE INDUSTRIAL REVOLUTION OF THE 18th CENTURY IN ENGLAND. 8vo. 10s. 6d.

TREVELYAN (Sir G. O., Bart.).—THE LIFE AND LETTERS OF LORD MACAULAY.

Popular Edition. Crown 8vo. 2s. 6d. | Cabinet Edition, 2 vols. Cr. 8vo. 12s.
Student's Edition. Crown 8vo. 6s. | Library Edition, 2 vols. 8vo. 36s.

———— THE EARLY HISTORY OF CHARLES JAMES FOX. Library Edition, 8vo. 18s. Cabinet Edition, Crown 8vo. 6s.

TROLLOPE (Anthony).—THE WARDEN. Cr. 8vo. 1s. bds., 1s. 6d. cl.

———— BARCHESTER TOWERS. Crown 8vo. 1s. boards, 1s. 6d. cloth.

VILLE (G.).—THE PERPLEXED FARMER: How is he to meet Alien Competition? Crown 8vo. 5s.

VIRGIL.—PUBLI VERGILI MARONIS BUCOLICA, GEORGICA, ÆNEIS; the Works of VIRGIL, Latin Text, with English Commentary and Index. By B. H. KENNEDY. Crown 8vo. 10s. 6d.

———— THE ÆNEID OF VIRGIL. Translated into English Verse. By John Conington. Crown 8vo. 6s.

———— THE POEMS OF VIRGIL. Translated into English Prose. By John Conington. Crown 8vo. 6s.

———— THE ECLOGUES AND GEORGICS OF VIRGIL. Translated from the Latin by J. W. Mackail. Printed on Dutch Hand-made Paper. 16mo. 5s.

WAKEMAN (H. O.) and HASSALL (A.).—ESSAYS INTRODUCTORY TO THE STUDY OF ENGLISH CONSTITUTIONAL HISTORY. Edited by H. O. WAKEMAN and A. HASSALL. Crown 8vo. 6s.

WALKER (A. Campbell-).—THE CORRECT CARD; or, How to Play at Whist; a Whist Catechism. Fcp. 8vo. 2s. 6d.

WALPOLE (Spencer).—HISTORY OF ENGLAND FROM THE CONCLUSION OF THE GREAT WAR IN 1815 to 1858. Library Edition. 5 vols. 8vo. £4 10s. Cabinet Edition. 6 vols. Crown 8vo. 6s. each.

WELLINGTON.—LIFE OF THE DUKE OF WELLINGTON. By the Rev. G. R. GLEIG. Crown 8vo. 3s. 6d.

WENDT (Ernest Emil).—PAPERS ON MARITIME LEGISLATION, with a Translation of the German Mercantile Laws relating to Maritime Commerce. Royal 8vo. £1 11s. 6d.

WEYMAN (Stanley J.).—THE HOUSE OF THE WOLF: a Romance. Crown 8vo. 6s.

WHATELY (E. Jane).—ENGLISH SYNONYMS. Edited by Archbishop WHATELY. Fcp. 8vo. 3s.

———— LIFE AND CORRESPONDENCE OF ARCHBISHOP WHATELY. With Portrait. Crown 8vo. 10s. 6d.

WHATELY (Archbishop).—ELEMENTS OF LOGIC. Cr. 8vo. 4s. 6d.

———— ELEMENTS OF RHETORIC. Crown 8vo. 4s. 6d.

———— LESSONS ON REASONING. Fcp. 8vo. 1s. 6d.

———— BACON'S ESSAYS, with Annotations. 8vo. 10s. 6d.

WILCOCKS (J. C.).—THE SEA FISHERMAN. Comprising the Chief Methods of Hook and Line Fishing in the British and other Seas, and Remarks on Nets, Boats, and Boating. Profusely Illustrated. Crown 8vo. 6s.

WILLICH (Charles M.).—POPULAR TABLES for giving Information for ascertaining the value of Lifehold, Leasehold, and Church Property, the Public Funds, &c. Edited by H. BENCE JONES. Crown 8vo. 10s. 6d.

WILLOUGHBY (Captain Sir John C.).—EAST AFRICA AND ITS BIG GAME. Illustrated by G. D. Giles and Mrs. Gordon Hake. Royal 8vo. 21s.

WITT (Prof.)—Works by. Translated by Frances Younghusband.

———— THE TROJAN WAR. Crown 8vo. 2s.

———— MYTHS OF HELLAS; or, Greek Tales. Crown 8vo. 3s. 6d.

———— THE WANDERINGS OF ULYSSES. Crown 8vo. 3s. 6d.

———— THE RETREAT OF THE TEN THOUSAND; being the Story of Xenophon's 'Anabasis'. With Illustrations. Crown 8vo. 3s. 6d.

WOLFF (Henry W.).—RAMBLES IN THE BLACK FOREST. Crown 8vo. 7s. 6d.

———— THE WATERING PLACES OF THE VOSGES. With Map. Crown 8vo. 4s. 6d.

———— THE COUNTRY OF THE VOSGES. With a Map. 8vo. 12s.

WOOD (Rev. J. G.).—HOMES WITHOUT HANDS; a Description of the Habitations of Animals. With 140 Illustrations. 8vo. 10s. 6d.

———— INSECTS AT HOME; a Popular Account of British Insects, their Structure, Habits, and Transformations. With 700 Illustrations. 8vo. 10s. 6d.

———— INSECTS ABROAD; a Popular Account of Foreign Insects, their Structure, Habits, and Transformations. With 600 Illustrations. 8vo. 10s. 6d.

———— BIBLE ANIMALS; a Description of every Living Creature mentioned in the Scriptures. With 112 Illustrations. 8vo. 10s. 6d.

———— STRANGE DWELLINGS; abridged from 'Homes without Hands'. With 60 Illustrations. Crown 8vo. 3s. 6d.

———— OUT OF DOORS; a Selection of Original Articles on Practical Natural History. With 11 Illustrations. Crown 8vo. 3s. 6d.

———— PETLAND REVISITED. With 33 Illustrations. Crown 8vo. 3s. 6d.

WORDSWORTH (Bishop Charles).—ANNALS OF MY EARLY LIFE, 1806-1846. 8vo. 15s.

WYLIE (J. H.).—HISTORY OF ENGLAND UNDER HENRY THE FOURTH. Crown 8vo. Vol. I. 10s. 6d. ; Vol. II.

YOUATT (William).—THE HORSE. With numerous Woodcuts. 8vo. 7s. 6d.

———— THE DOG. With numerous Woodcuts. 8vo. 6s.

ZELLER (Dr. E.).—HISTORY OF ECLECTICISM IN GREEK PHILO-SOPHY. Translated by Sarah F. Alleyne. Crown 8vo. 10s. 6d.

———— THE STOICS, EPICUREANS, AND SCEPTICS. Translated by the Rev. O. J. Reichel. Crown 8vo. 15s.

———— SOCRATES AND THE SOCRATIC SCHOOLS. Translated by the Rev. O. J. Reichel. Crown 8vo. 10s. 6d.

———— PLATO AND THE OLDER ACADEMY. Translated by Sarah F. Alleyne and Alfred Goodwin. Crown 8vo. 18s.

———— THE PRE-SOCRATIC SCHOOLS. Translated by Sarah F. Alleyne. 2 vols. Crown 8vo. 30s.

———— OUTLINES OF THE HISTORY OF GREEK PHILOSOPHY. Translated by Sarah F. Alleyne and Evelyn Abbott. Crown 8vo. 10s. 6d.

50,000—10/91.   ABERDEEN UNIVERSITY PRESS,

www.ingramcontent.com/pod-product-compliance
Lightning Source LLC
Chambersburg PA
CBHW030643030726
47497CB00006B/1927